AMY'S PROMISE

BERNICE THURMAN HUNTER

AMY'S PROMISE

COVER BY
TONY MEERS

Scholastic Canada Ltd.

Scholastic Canada Ltd.
175 Hillmount Road, Markham, Ontario L6C 1Z7

Scholastic Inc.
555 Broadway, New York, NY 10012, USA

Scholastic Australia Pty Limited
PO Box 579, Gosford, NSW 2250, Australia

Scholastic New Zealand Limited
Private Bag 94407, Greenmount, Auckland, New Zealand

Scholastic Ltd.
Villiers House, Clarendon Avenue, Leamington Spa,
Warwickshire CV32 5PR, UK

*Thanks to Len Read and Florence White
for the use of their mother's picture*

Canadian Cataloguing in Publication Data

Hunter, Bernice Thurman
    Amy's promise

ISBN 0-590-24621-6

I. Title.

PS8565.U577A82 1995   jC813'.54   C95-930984-5
PZ7.H85Am 1995

9 8 7 6 5 4   Printed and bound in Canada   0 1 2 3 4 / 0
                    Manufactured by Webcom Limited

Contents

To Annette, with love.

Chapter 1

Amy Phair

Amy Phair finished setting the kitchen table, then slid into the chair next to her grandmother.

Across the green-checkered oilcloth, her three brothers were lined up in a row: eleven-year-old Mikey — just one year younger than Amy — nine-year-old Patty and seven-year-old Harry.

The big armchair at the head of the table was still empty. But the mixing bowl full of savoury stew, and the stack of buttered bread beside it, were placed within easy reach.

"Can we start now? I'm starved," whined young Harry. He was always next to tears when he was hungry.

"No, Harry, wait for Daddy," Amy warned.

Gramma sniffed. "He'll keep us waiting till it's all gone cold," she complained.

Amy glanced through the kitchen door into the

parlour. The door to her father's den was still closed, so she pinched a slice of bread from the bottom of the pile and gave it to Harry. The rest of the stack tilted, then tumbled over.

Just then the den door banged open and out lumbered John Phair, his clothes dishevelled, his black hair standing on end, red-faced and bleary-eyed.

As quickly as she could, with her rheumatic fingers, Gramma Davis began re-building the pyramid of bread.

"What's going on out here? Who spilled the bread?" demanded their father as he sat down with a thump in the armchair.

The piece of bread trembled in Harry's hand.

"Can you not wait for the breadwinner before you start stuffing yourself?" growled their father. "Where's your manners, you greedy little sod?" His arm shot out like a spring, catching Harry's hand, and the bread went flying. It skimmed off Gramma's forehead and dropped silently to the floor.

The three boys sat stock still, and Gramma Davis seemed to shrivel under his gaze. But Amy looked her father right in the eye. "It was an accident, Daddy. Besides, I gave Harry the bread. He was hungry and you were late for supper."

"Well, blast you then!" he hollered. "Blast all of

you, ungrateful varmints that you are!"

At that moment, out of the corner of her eye, Amy caught a glimpse of a pale face through the flimsy curtain on the window of the kitchen door. The muscles in her stomach tightened as she recognized her new friend, Winnie Plum.

Amy darted her eyes back to her father. His face was still red with anger as he slopped stew onto his plate, berating his family with every scoopful.

Without moving her head, Amy slid her eyes back to the window. She breathed a sigh of relief to see that Winnie was gone.

ᨅ   ᨅ   ᨅ

That night Amy went to bed early. That was the one good thing about being the only girl in the family: she had her own bedroom, where she could be alone. It was a small but cosy room with only three pieces of furniture in it: a double bed that filled half the room, a washstand with a Tiffany lamp on it . . . her mother's lamp . . . and a dresser with a mirror, cloudy where the silver had worn off the back. The room had no closet, so most of her clothes were in the dresser drawers and her three dresses hung on the back of the door.

Pulling the chain of the lamp, she picked up a small oval frame from the washstand. In it was a hand-painted snapshot of her mother. The picture was a bit blurry but Amy found that if she stared at it long and hard enough she could make her mother's face come into focus and their eyes would meet.

With her fingertip, Amy traced the outline of her mother's cloud of brown hair, then her slim figure in her pink flowered dress. She kissed the cool glass and whispered, "Goodnight, Mama!"

Replacing the picture on the washstand, she switched off the light and lay back on her pillow. Quickly, before her mother's image began to fade, Amy struggled to remember the time when her mother was alive.

Snatches of memories flitted through her mind like butterflies: helping her mother bathe baby Jane in the white oval tub on the table; holding the baby on her lap, swaddled in a white towel, while her mother threw the bath water out into the garden; leaning her elbows on her mother's knee as she nursed the baby.

She remembered the fresh smell of her mother's long brown hair as she brushed it dry in the sun, and the fragrance of lavender coming from her mother's nightdress when she climbed into bed beside her on a Sunday morning. She remembered her mother's beautiful eyes (the colour of spring violets, her father used to say) smiling down at her.

Amy's last memory of those violet-blue eyes was the day her mother died. The whole family stood silently around the deathbed. Amy was at the far end, clinging to the brass post.

"Amy." Her mother's voice was a breathless whisper as she held out her thin white hand. The others moved back as Amy crept forward. She put her own plump little hand into her mother's and felt her mother's tight grip on her fingers. Her mother's eyes were sunken into deep dark hollows. "Come closer," she whispered. Amy climbed onto the bed and leaned so near that she felt a wisp of sickly-sweet breath on her cheek.

"Amy . . . I want you to promise me something."

"Yes, Mama."

"Watch over the little ones for me. You're the oldest, so I'll leave them in your keeping. Promise me, daughter?"

Not really understanding at all, six-year-old Amy Phair replied, "I promise, Mama."

Almost instantly she felt her mother's hand go limp. Then her long black lashes fell like a curtain over her eyes. And she slept, never to waken again.

Twelve-year-old Amy shivered at the memory. But one memory triggered another and she couldn't seem to stop them. She saw her mother's glassed-in coffin in front of the parlour window, strewn with pink and red paper hearts because it was Valentine's Day. Gramma Davis always said, Nonsense, Lavinia's coffin was not glassed-in, and there were no paper hearts. But that's what Amy remembered.

The last recollection of that awful February day in 1920 still haunted Amy's dreams: she was sitting far back in the corner of the big leather rocking chair, her black-buttoned boots just reaching the edge of the seat, when someone placed the baby on her lap. Baby Jane was wrapped in a white blanket like a cocoon, a pink knitted cap on her head, sucking on a soother.

Aunt Bessie and Uncle Wallace were pulling on their winter coats with the black mourning bands sewn on the left sleeves. They had travelled all the way from Winnipeg, Manitoba, for the funeral. Then Aunt Bessie came towards Amy, a sad smile on her pudgy face, leaned over and lifted the baby out of her arms.

There was a tearful goodbye at the door, then they were gone.

Heaving a deep sigh, Amy sat up in bed, switched on the light again and got a little notebook out of the washstand drawer. Gramma had found the notebook one day when she opened a fresh can of Estabrooks tea. It had been on top of the tea-leaves, sealed in cellophane. "May I have it, Gramma?" Amy had begged.

"I suppose so. It's no earthly use to me," Gramma had said. Amy had kept it ever since. She called it her T-book and in it she wrote messages to her mother.

Opening it where a pencil on a string marked the page, she licked the pencil's black tip and began.

"Feb. 18, 1926.

"Dear Mama, today I am very sad because it is six years since you went away. I wish I had a sister to talk to. Oh, Mama, why did you have to die? And why did Daddy let Aunt Bessie take our baby? Didn't he love her anymore? Maybe he doesn't love any of us. Maybe that's why he's so cross all the time. I hope he never sends Harry away. That was the worst part, Mama. That you and baby Jane both disappeared on the same day.

"Sorrowfully, Amy Phair."

Chapter 2

Winnie Plum

*E*very morning before Amy set off for school she had to help her grandmother with the dishes. "Why can't Mikey take a turn?" she complained. "He's just as big as I am."

"Don't be foolish," Gramma snapped, handing her another soapy bowl to wipe. "Washing up is woman's work." Then she glanced out the steamy window over the sink. "Who's that girl standing on our porch in the rain?" she said, lifting the corner of the curtain with a wet finger.

Amy stretched her neck to see over the plants on the window sill. "Oh, that's my new friend, Winnie Plum. Her family just moved in the next street over." Amy waved the tea towel at Winnie. "Can she come in and stand on the mat, Gramma?"

"I suppose so. She'll catch her death of cold out there. It's queer weather we're having for

February. I'd rather see snow than rain. It's more natural."

Amy flung open the kitchen door, smiled at Winnie, and pointed to the doormat that Gramma had braided out of old lisle stockings.

Winnie waited dutifully, dripping onto the mat. Her blue wool coat, with the rabbit collar and hat to match, were misty with rain. Dewdrops glistened on the tips of her long gold ringlets and her cheeks were rosy and shiny as apples.

Peering over her steel-rimmed spectacles, Gramma Davis looked her up and down. "Haven't you got an umbrella, girl?" she demanded.

"Yes, but it wasn't raining when I left," answered Winnie.

"Humph!" muttered Gramma.

Young Harry was waiting impatiently, his red tuque pulled down over his eyebrows. He was not allowed to walk to school alone yet. "C'mon, Amy," he begged. "If I'm late Miss Small will smack my bottom."

Amy wiped the last bowl and hung the towel on the wooden spokes above the stove. Then she got her brown coat and tam from the cellarway and took Harry's red-mittened hand.

They were on their way out the door when Gramma called, "Don't forget your galoshes! My word, you'd forget your head if it wasn't tacked on. And you may take my umbrella if you promise not to lose it. Now away you go — and behave yourselves." She patted the crown of Winnie's fur-trimmed hat as they went out the door.

Huddled under the big black umbrella, the three children scurried up the street.

"Your granny's nice," remarked Winnie.

Amy thought about all the dishes the boys didn't have to do, and the affectionate pat on Winnie's head. Squinching up her nose she said, "No, she's not. She's just putting on a show."

The rain had stopped so Harry let go of Amy's hand and sprinted on ahead. Amy collapsed the big umbrella and hooked it over her arm.

"Winnie . . . "

"Yes, Amy."

"You know last night, when you looked in our window . . . "

"I didn't hear a thing, honest," said Winnie quickly.

"You must have. My dad's voice is awful loud when he's mad."

"Well, I ran off as soon as I saw you were eating your supper," Winnie insisted. "But . . . why was your dad mad, Amy?" Then she added hastily, "You don't have to tell me if you don't want to."

"Oh," Amy shrugged. "He's been mad ever since my mother died."

"Your mother died!" Winnie gasped. "Oh, I'm sorry, Amy. When did it happen?"

"A long time ago."

They were just turning into the schoolyard and the bell was already ringing. Amy was glad, because, much as she liked her new friend, she wasn't sure how much she wanted to tell her yet.

The first thing Amy saw when she got settled at her desk was the strange name scrawled in huge letters across the blackboard under the grade and date: "JUNIOR FOURTH CLASS, FEBRUARY 28, 1926. MRS. B. HARDACRE."

"Where's Mr. Daniels?" she whispered across the aisle to Rupert White.

"He's away. I heard he took awful sick in the night."

"Oh!" cried Amy. "I hope he comes back soon."

Suddenly the teacher looked up. She had sharp little eyes, a hawk-like face and a big black nest of a bun perched on top of her head. "Who's talking?" she demanded.

Rupert obligingly pointed to Amy.

"What's your name, girl?"

"Amy Phair."

"Stand when you speak."

Amy stood and repeated her name.

Mrs. Hardacre ran her finger down the list on the desk in front of her. "Oh, you're the girl that has no mother," she said flatly. "You may sit down."

Amy felt her legs turn to water as she sank into her seat. Her heart throbbed and blood rushed to her face. She had to bite her bottom lip to stop its quivering.

She heard Winnie gasp behind her, and a hush fell over the classroom. But the teacher didn't seem to notice as she began the lesson. "Open your Arithmetic books to page 49," she instructed, "and solve the first five problems." Everybody set to work. Everybody except Amy. She sat staring, her mind blank, and she had to stay in at recess because her page was empty. The rest of a day went by in a blur.

Chapter 3

The House on Silvertree

On the way home, Winnie took Amy's hand. "Do you want to come over to my house, Amy, and meet my mother?"

"I'd love to, Winnie," Amy said. "But I'll have to take Harry home first and ask Gramma's permission."

As they turned up the walk leading to the back porch of the frame house on Wheeler Street, Winnie said, "I like the colour of your house, Amy. I never saw a purple house before."

Amy laughed a bit ruefully. "My dad painted it violet to match my mother's eyes. It used to be pretty, but the weather has changed the violet to purple. Most people think it's ugly now."

"Well, I think it's pretty."

"Gee, thanks, Winnie."

The kitchen was empty when they stepped inside the door. Amy and Winnie stopped on the mat so they wouldn't have to take off their galoshes.

"Gramma, I'm home!" called Amy.

Gramma Davis came puffing up the cellar stairs carrying a big yellow turnip and a six-quart basket of potatoes. "Where's your brother?" she asked querulously.

"He's out in the yard making a snowman." The weather had turned cold again and the rain had changed to sleet, then snow. "Gramma . . . "

Gramma Davis tumbled the vegetables into the tin sink and began pumping water over them. Then she knocked sharply on the window with her wide gold wedding band and beckoned to Harry. He came in obediently and squeezed between Amy and Winnie on the mat.

Gramma knelt down to pull off his boots. "You know you mustn't play in your school clothes, you young scamp. Now run along and change into your play-clothes." She gave his bottom an affectionate pat as he ran by.

"Gramma . . . "

"For mercy sakes, girl, can't you see I'm busy? What is it this time?"

"Winnie wants me to come to her house to meet

her mother, don't you, Winnie?"

"Yes." Winnie bobbed her curly head. "That's what Mama said just this morning. Bring your new friend home for supper, she said."

Gramma frowned at the sink full of vegetables. "I'll need help with the supper here. And I'm not halfway through the ironing. I've only got two hands, you know."

"I'll only stay a little while, Gramma," said Amy eagerly. "I promise I'll be back in time to help with supper. And I can finish the ironing after supper."

Gramma turned and looked at them both with pursed lips. Then she surprised Amy by reaching out and tucking her straight brown hair into each side of her woolen tam. Then she dampened the corner of her apron in the sink and gave Amy's round face a lick-and-a-promise.

"How far away do you live?" Gramma asked Winnie.

"Only the next street over, Mrs. Phair."

Gramma's hand shot up like a stop sign. "Before you say another word, let's get one thing straight. I am *not* Mrs. Phair. I am Mrs. Davis. I am no blood relation to that one in there!" She pointed into the parlour at the closed door of Amy's father's den.

"I'm sorry, Mrs. Davis. I didn't know."

"Of course you didn't. But see that you don't

make the same mistake twice. Now away you go. And Amy . . . don't be late, mind!"

"I won't, Gramma. Thank you, Gramma!"

Hand in hand they raced through the alleyway between the houses that led to Silvertree Boulevard. Laughing breathlessly, they collapsed on the front steps of Winnie's veranda.

"Your granny doesn't like your dad much, does she?" Winnie ventured to say.

"No." Amy turned to her new friend and searched deep into her eyes. "If I tell you something . . . something very private . . . will you promise to keep it a secret forever?"

"Yes, Amy. I solemnly promise." Winnie crossed her heart so sincerely that Amy knew she could trust her.

So Amy told Winnie everything about how her mother had died on Valentine's Day six years before, about the deathbed promise she had made, about her father's broken heart and what had happened to her baby sister.

"I think my gramma blames my father for everything," Amy said, "but I'm not sure why."

"Oh, I'm sorry, Amy." Winnie moved closer and put her arm around Amy's shoulders. Then she asked in a whisper, "What was your mother like, Amy?"

Amy sighed and shook her head. "I never really knew my mother, Winnie. But I've missed her all my life."

"But how can you miss somebody you never knew?"

Suddenly Amy jumped to her feet and changed the subject. "Are you allowed to go in your front door?" she asked.

"Sure." Winnie leapt up and flung open the door. "Mama! Mama!" she called. "Look who's here!"

Amy was surprised to see that the front door of Winnie's house led down a long hall to the kitchen. The front door of the purple house opened right up into the parlour.

Winnie's mother, a tall woman with a laughing face and shingled brown hair, appeared at the kitchen door. Winnie ran straight down the hall runner in her snowy overshoes, right into her mother's arms.

Suddenly Amy felt shy. Mrs. Plum gave her daughter a big hug and a kiss, then they both turned towards Amy.

"Mama, this is Amy Phair. She's my new best friend."

"Well, hello dear! Don't just stand there, come in, come in."

Unbuckling her galoshes, Amy set them side by

side on the welcome mat and walked down the long hall.

Two sets of glass doors led off the hall. Amy took a quick glance into the rooms as she passed. Through the diamond-shaped windows of the first set of doors she saw a chesterfield suite, a fireplace and a floor lamp. The second door opened onto the dining room. In the centre was a big oval table surrounded by high-backed chairs with leather seats. In the corner by the window was an upright piano with a goose-necked lamp on top.

All of a sudden Mrs. Plum cried, "Oh, my stars!" and Amy jumped as if she had been caught spying.

Wrapping a dishtowel around her hand, Mrs. Plum snatched a bubbling saucepan off the stove just as it was about to boil over. Setting it aside, she said, "Take off your coats and hang them up. And there's Mittens scratching at the door. Let her in before she freezes her pink paddies off."

Winnie opened the kitchen door and in strutted a pure white cat with four black paws that looked like woolen mittens.

"Oh!" Amy cried and dropped to her knees. Mittens arched her back, purring loudly, and bunted her wet nose on Amy's face.

Mrs. Plum filled two large mugs with frothy cocoa and set them on the table beside a cookie jar shaped like a rooster. "Help yourselves while I go fetch the baby. He must be awake by now."

Winnie lifted off the rooster's head and got them each an oatmeal cookie. Sitting at the table, sipping hot cocoa and munching on her cookie, Amy had never felt so cosy. Not even in her own bed. The kitchen was warm from the stove, the cocoa and cookie were delicious, and Mittens rubbed back and forth across her ribbed stockings underneath the table.

Presently Mrs. Plum returned, cuddling a chubby, bald-headed baby. "This is Pauley," she said, leaning down to show him off to Amy.

"Polly? Winnie said she had a brother."

Mrs. Plum laughed. "Well, she told the truth. His name is Paul, after his father; I wanted to call him Junior but my husband wouldn't hear of it so Winnie nicknamed him Pauley."

Amy's cocoa grew cold as she watched Mrs. Plum dress Pauley. The baby wiggled and gurgled and squealed and turned upside-down like an acrobat on his mother's lap. Mrs. Plum laughed as she struggled to squeeze him into his rompers.

Winnie was busy playing with Mittens, but Amy couldn't take her eyes off the baby. Suddenly she had a memory flash of her own mother dressing Janey on her lap — the smell of baby powder on velvety skin and the feel of silky baby hair.

Mrs. Plum was just about to tuck Pauley into his high-chair when Amy's arms shot out.

"Would you like to hold him, dear? I'm afraid he's a bit of a handful."

"Oh, I don't mind." Amy assured her. "I've been taking care of our Harry since he was two years old and he's as bad as can be sometimes."

Mrs. Plum laughed, popped a rubber dummy into the baby's mouth and handed him over to Amy. Amy hugged Pauley tight and gazed into his round blue eyes.

"How old is Pauley, Mrs. Plum?" she asked.

"He turned six months old on Valentine's Day," replied Mrs. Plum.

Valentine's Day! Amy gave a sudden gasp that made Winnie look up. Dropping the cat, Winnie jumped to her feet and cried, "Would you like to see my room, Amy?"

"Yes please," whispered Amy.

So Mrs. Plum took the baby and Winnie grabbed Amy's hand and led her down the hall and up the staircase.

Winnie's room was beautiful: the pink-flowered organdy curtains, the counterpane and the canopy over the bed all matched. Winnie had her own desk, too, and a bookshelf and a white-enamel clock, shaped like a daisy, on the wall.

The clock read twenty-five minutes past four.

"Oh, my goodness!" Amy got a sudden picture of the turnip floating in the sink. "I have to go, Winnie. If I'm late Gramma won't let me come back again."

She ran all the way home and stumbled in the kitchen door just as the mantle clock in the parlour chimed half past four.

Chapter 4

Easter Holidays

*I*t seemed to Amy that Valentine's Day was no sooner over than along came Easter, and she hated Easter almost as much as Valentine's Day.

It wasn't the church service that she hated, or the school holidays. It was just that Easter holidays weren't really holidays at all, because that's when Gramma did the spring cleaning.

"Put your dustcap on and let's get started," said Gramma. But that was one thing Amy refused to do. "You'll be sorry when your hair is full of cobwebs," warned Gramma. But Amy stuck to her guns. No dustcap.

Gramma sent the boys out to play and she and Amy set to work. They stripped the beds and took down the curtains and emptied the cupboards and beat the carpets over the backyard line.

Day after day they dusted and swept until every

nook and cranny of the house had been scrubbed and scoured. All except Amy's father's room. Gramma had tried to clean it once and got chased out and sworn at for her pains.

Then at night, after the boys had been sent off to bed, Amy helped with the mending.

"Thread my needles." Gramma pushed the wicker sewing-basket across the table towards Amy. It was Amy's job to keep the needles threaded and knotted and stuck into the sawdust pincushion ready for use.

She didn't resent this job so much because she felt sorry for her grandmother. The doctor had said that Gramma had something in her eyes called cataracts and that's why she couldn't see very well. Still Gramma did her best; she turned shirt collars and cuffs inside-out, mended all the stockings, and replaced the red ribbons on Amy's straw hat with new blue ones.

"There." Gramma took off her spectacles and rubbed her tired eyes. "Now the whole lot of you are ready for the Easter Parade." She sighed with satisfaction.

Amy closed the sewing-basket with a sharp click. "I'm not going to the parade, Gramma," she said.

"What? After me sewing new ribbons on your straw bonnet?"

"But what I really need is new shoes," Amy protested.

"You need no such thing," snapped Gramma. "I had Mikey take all the shoes to the shoemaker just last week for soles and heels. And I even got you brand-new laces. So why on earth would you need new shoes?"

"Because they're not shoes, Gramma, they're high-laced boots and they're ugly and old-fashioned. I'm the only girl in my class who still wears boots. It's humiliating and I'm not going to wear them to the Easter Parade."

"Humiliating my foot!" Waving her hand impatiently, Gramma accidentally knocked the sewing-basket off the edge of the table.

It landed with a crash and the lid flew open, spewing the contents all over the parlour floor.

"Now see what you made me do with your high-faluting ways!" cried Gramma, her rheumy eyes filling with angry tears. "You get down there and start picking up this minute." Wringing her knobbly hands she moaned, "Every bone in my body aches with rheumatism."

Amy could see by the pain on her grandmother's face that it was true, so she got down on her hands and knees and began retrieving the twirling buttons and spools of thread and the scattered pins and needles. They stuck into her fingers and brought tears to her eyes.

Suddenly the front door burst open and in blew John Phair on a gust of wind. Because the door to his den had been shut all night it had not occurred to either of them to wonder where he was.

"What's all this?" he demanded, kicking the loose spools out of his way. "What are you doing down there, Vinny?"

Her father often called her Vinny because her second name was Lavinia, after her mother.

"Gramma spilled the basket and I'm picking up," she answered, keeping her head down to hide the tears. But he must have heard the tremor in her voice because he turned his bad temper on Gramma.

"What did you do to her this time, you old varmint?" he sniped.

Amy jumped up and set the basket on the table. Then she stood between her grandmother and her father and looked him straight in the eye. "It was an accident, Daddy," she said.

"Then why are you crying, Vinny? What did she say to upset you?"

"It wasn't anything Gramma said. It's just that I'm tired. And I don't want to go to the Easter Parade."

"Why not? Haven't you got a spring bonnet?"

"Oh, yes." She put the wide-brimmed straw hat on over her cobwebby hair (Gramma had been right about the dustcap) and tied the new ribbons under her chin.

Her father looked at her speechless for a moment. Then he said, "You look almost comely in that nice bonnet. Why don't you want to show it off at the parade?"

"Because . . . " Amy glanced at Gramma who was hunched over the pincushion nervously poking in stray pins and needles. "I'll show you, Daddy," she said, and ran upstairs.

She came back down carrying the high-laced boots with the ugly red felt lining. "These are all the shoes I've got and they're as out-of-fashion as laced corsets. The girls all laugh at me and I hate them."

She held her breath as he took the boots in his big hands and looked them over. "There's a lot of good wear left in these here boots," he said, and she felt a wave of disappointment. Then he spun around on his heel, marched to the front door and threw the boots out into the night.

Brushing his hands together he said, "There, good riddance to bad rubbish. Tomorrow I'll take you downtown to Eaton's and get you your Easter shoes. Now go to bed and quit your bawling."

He stomped into his den and was just about to close the door when he stopped short and poked his head back out. "You've still got a father, you know," he said. Then he shut the door behind him.

Amy stood for a moment looking at the closed door. Sometimes she didn't know what to make of her father. Shaking her head she turned to Gramma, and their eyes met. They didn't speak, but both pairs of eyes were swimming with tired tears. Amy took off the bonnet and put it on the table.

Then, very quietly so her father wouldn't hear, she went out the front door, found her boots where they had landed on the purple veranda steps and took them back up to her room. Then she came back down and washed the cobwebs out of her hair at the kitchen sink.

The very next day, true to his word, her father marched her downtown to Eaton's and gave her the pick of the shoe department. She chose the most beautiful shoes she could find: grey suede slippers with a strap across the instep that fastened onto a real pearl button.

On Easter Sunday, after church, Amy and Winnie joined the Easter Parade on the rumbling boardwalk. Amy was sure everyone in the crowd was noticing her new suede slippers. Even Winnie, who wore a brand new Easter outfit, said she had never seen such gorgeous shoes in all her life.

ða ða ða

On the first day of school after the Easter holidays Amy was about to leave with Harry when her grandmother remarked, "You're wearing your boots, I see. Aren't you afraid of being humiliated?"

Amy felt a sharp retort on the tip of her tongue. Then she saw the quirk of a smile at the corners of Gramma's crepe-paper lips.

So Amy smiled back. "I've decided to save my new shoes for Sunday best," she said.

"That's a good girl," Gramma nodded her head approvingly. "And when summer comes I'll see that you get new running shoes, to boot."

Amy couldn't remember her grandmother ever calling her a good girl before. Her heart felt as light as a feather in the wind. She waved to Winnie who was waiting on the front sidewalk. "Come on, Harry," she cried, "There's a good boy." She grabbed his hand, and they practically flew all the way to school.

Chapter 5

The Quack

Amy was a good student and she really liked school, especially this year with Mr. Daniels for her teacher. She was pretty sure she was his favourite, and she tried not to miss a day.

But one rainy April morning, as she sat at the breakfast table, Gramma said, "Young Harry's burning up with fever, Amy. You'll have to stay home to help me nurse him. I can't do it alone, with my rheumatics."

Amy sighed her disappointment and ate her porridge sullenly.

After Mike and Pat had gone off to school, Amy helped Gramma pull open the davenport in the parlour and they made Harry's bed there to save running up and down stairs all day long.

Gramma fed Harry beef broth to thicken his blood and showed Amy how to sponge him with lukewarm water to lower his fever. Then she dosed him up with epsom salts to clean the poison out of his system and put a mustard plaster on his chest to clear his passageways. But in spite of all their loving ministrations poor little Harry got worse and worse. A terrible cough racked his body and his face was red and glistening with sweat.

Feeling his forehead anxiously, Amy said to her grandmother, "I think he needs the doctor." Maybe the doctor's medicine would work quicker than the homemade remedy Gramma had made out of turpentine and brown sugar.

Gramma laid her papery cheek on Harry's feverish forehead. "He's not so bad that I can't doctor him myself," she decided. "After all, didn't I raise seven children without the help of modern medicine?"

Oh, sure, Amy thought darkly. But what about the little ones you lost?

But by nightfall Harry was no better, so Gramma decided he should stay on the davenport, which had been her own bed since she'd come to live with them.

"The boys' room is too draughty," she explained, "and I don't want Mike and Pat catching the fever; so I shall have to sleep with you, Amy."

Sleep with *her!* Amy clapped her hand over her

mouth to stop from screaming. She wouldn't have minded sharing with a sister, but not with Gramma!

Her room had always been her sanctuary and she guarded it as fiercely as a lion guards its den. Once she had caught Mike and Pat jumping on her bed. She had a pair of scissors in her hand because she had just cut out a calendar picture to hang on her wall.

Pat was sailing up towards the ceiling and Mike was crouching for his next launch when she let the scissors fly. *Zing* they went, like an arrow, missing the boys by inches. The points of the scissors stuck with a twang into the dresser on the other side of the room.

Screaming, the boys ran from the room.

Oh, no! Amy thought, I'm in trouble now. But to her amazement her brothers had not told on her. They probably knew their father would wallop them for ruining the bedsprings.

Since then no-one had ever come into her room, not even Gramma Davis since it was Amy's job to clean the upstairs bedrooms on Saturdays. But now Gramma was going to *sleep* with her! How could she stop her? Harry would just have to get better in a hurry.

That night Amy went to bed early, exhausted and angry. Getting her T-book out of the drawer she opened it and wrote, "Dearest Mama, Help! Gramma is going to sleep with me and I don't think I can bear it! Your distracted daughter, Amy Phair."

❧ ❧ ❧

Amy woke from a fitful sleep when the mantle clock struck one and she heard her father come in from work. He was on the graveyard shift this week, from four to midnight. She heard Gramma say, "You'll have to keep an eye on the boy, John. I've got to get some rest. I'm plumb tuckered out from nursing him."

There was no reply from her father, but a few minutes later the old woman came wheezing up the stairs.

Amy heard her petticoats rustle as she undressed in the dark. Her teeth gurgled as they sank to the bottom of a glass of salt water on the washstand, and her knees creaked as she knelt to say her prayers. Then, heaving a great sigh, she finally crawled into bed beside Amy.

Amy clung to the far side of the felt mattress, but the bed sagged in the middle and soon Gramma's bony back was pressed up against hers. Amy tried to pull herself as far away as she could get.

"Be still!" commanded Gramma irritably. "How can a body sleep with you wiggling like that?"

Amy didn't make a sound, but the tears rolled down her face and soaked into the pillow.

She didn't sleep a wink that night as she tried desperately to keep from touching Gramma.

❧ ❧ ❧

The next day Harry was much worse. Moaning and thrashing he began to talk gibberish. "Snakes!" he screamed, slapping wildly at the blanket. "Get them away! Take them offa me!"

"Oh, my soul, he's gone delirious," cried Gramma, wringing her hands helplessly. "I guess there's nothing for it but the doctor." So she sent Mikey racing to Queen Street to tell Doctor Harris to come quick.

In the meantime, Amy tried to comfort her little brother. Giving the top blanket a good shake, she tucked it in around him and grabbed his flailing hands. They felt as hot and dry as toast.

"They're all gone now, Harry," Amy assured him. "I chased them all away."

Harry was a very sick boy, the doctor said, and he gave Gramma and Amy instructions how to care for him. He told Mike and Pat to be extra quiet and to stay as far away from their little brother as possible. "Put five drops of carbolic acid in a bucket of water and place it in the corner to disinfect the room," he ordered gravely. He came twice a day for the rest of the week to check on his patient.

On Saturday Doctor Harris was late arriving.

"I've had a busy afternoon bringing twins into the world," he told them proudly. Then he threw his hat and coat at the end of the pull-out bed and drew up a chair beside Harry. Leaning over, he pressed his ear to Harry's chest, then looked down his throat with a flat stick and said, "Say ah!" Harry gagged, "Aahh!" The doctor looked, then turned to Gramma. "He's passed the crisis now, Missus. He'll be right as rain in a day or two. But I'll leave you another bottle of medicine just to be on the safe side. When it's all gone you can let him up."

Opening his black bag he took out a bottle of Watkins' thick brown syrup and was just handing it to Gramma when the den door suddenly swung open and out stepped a shaggy-headed John Phair. It was the first time he'd seen the doctor, since he had sat up with Harry every night and slept all day. Nobody had told him that the doctor had been sent for.

Amy watched, mesmerized, as her father's face changed into the face of a madman.

"YOU!" he roared.

Lurching forward he knocked the bottle out of the doctor's hand and sent it smashing against the wall. "You . . . what murdered my wife and left me alone with five motherless children. Didn't I tell you never to darken my door again? What are you here for this time . . . to murder my son?"

Doctor Harris' face drained of colour. Side-stepping the madman he grabbed his bag off the floor and his coat from the bed and ran hatless out the door.

Gramma and Amy stood trembling and speechless. Harry began to whimper. Then John Phair leaned down so close to his mother-in-law's rigid face that his breath steamed up her spectacles. Jabbing his finger an inch from her nose he growled, "Don't you ever let that murdering quack what calls himself a doctor into my house again. Do you hear me, woman?"

"Daddy!" Amy squeezed herself between them, her heart hammering. "It's not Gramma's fault. It was my idea."

Out of the corner of her eye she saw Mike and Pat peering around the kitchen door, their eyes as big as saucers.

Her dad ran his fingers through his mop of black hair and dragged the palms of his hands down over his eyes and face. Waving them both wildly aside, he leaned over his son on the davenport.

"Are you all right now, lad?" he asked in a hoarse whisper.

"Yes, Daddy," Harry whispered back.

John Phair straightened up, turned, and noticed the doctor's felt fedora lying on the floor. Raising his foot, he mashed it flat with his big black boot. Then he stomped over to the wall-rack, threw on his overcoat and cap, and went slamming out the door.

⛧ ⛧ ⛧

That night Amy wrote in her T-book. "Dearest Mama: Harry is nearly better. Daddy is very angry. Gramma and I are tired. Amy."

She didn't even pretend to be asleep when her grandmother crawled wearily into bed beside her. Amy's eyes were wide open and had grown accustomed to the dark. Gramma was lying on her back, her bony body deflated like an airless balloon. Amy could see her sharp profile framed by the frill of her nightcap.

"Gramma . . . " she whispered.

"What is it?"

"Did the doctor really kill my mother?"

"No, lass."

"Then why did my father say that?"

Gramma drew in a long, wheezy breath and let it out on a fluttering sigh. "He's bound and determined to blame somebody," she answered bitterly. "Anybody but hisself." She was silent for a moment. "He even blames Lavinia at times."

Those last words brought back a shock of memory that charged like an electric current through Amy's body.

It was not long after her mother's death. Amy was still only six years old and for a reason she couldn't recall Gramma had taken the boys out somewhere and left her alone in the house.

Wandering around the quiet rooms, Amy had noticed that the door to her father's den was open a crack. She thought she heard him talking to someone, so she crept up to the door and peeked through the crack.

There stood her father, his hands clasped behind him, his head thrown back, staring up at the big oval portrait of her mother hanging on the wall.

Then she heard him say the most dreadful thing: "Damn you for dying, Vinny!" His voice was a terrible whisper and it sent cold shivers down Amy's spine.

Six years later, Amy still shivered with the memory.

Chapter 6

The King's Mail

*I*t was quiet in the house for some time after the doctor's visit. Even the boys were subdued, and Amy didn't hurry home from school.

"I wish I lived at your house, Winnie." Amy took off her woolen tam to let the warm spring breeze blow through her straight brown hair. "And I wish you were my sister." They stopped to let Harry catch up.

"Well, I haven't got a sister either, Amy," consoled Winnie.

"No, but you've got a cat and a baby."

"Well, the cat's okay but a baby brother can be a terrible nuisance sometimes."

"Huh!" scoffed Amy, giving Harry a playful cuff on the head. "Don't tell me about brothers."

"Have you got a picture of your baby sister, Amy?"

38

"No. And she's not a baby anymore. She's six years old now."

They slowed their steps as they got closer to the purple house, and young Harry ran on ahead.

Suddenly Amy's eyes lit up. "I've got a swell idea," she said. "I'm going to write to my Aunt Bessie and ask her for a picture of Janey. And then, as soon as Janey is old enough to read, I'll write to her myself." They stopped on the sidewalk in front of the purple house and continued talking.

"Will you show me the picture as soon as you get it, Amy?"

"Of course, Winnie. You'll be the first person to see it."

Out of the corner of her eye Amy noticed the curtain in the parlour window move and she saw Gramma Davis squinting through the glass.

"I have to go in now, Winnie. I'll see you tomorrow."

The minute she set foot on the kitchen mat Gramma snapped at her. "Why aren't you wearing your hat, you foolish girl? Are you trying to catch your death of cold and cause me more trouble?"

Amy pinched off her rubbers, flopped her schoolbag on the table, and hung up her coat and tam in the cellarway. "It's warm as spring today, Gramma," she said.

"Well, my rheumatism tells me otherwise," the old lady grumbled, rubbing her swollen knuckles. "And why didn't you invite your pretty little friend in for a bit?"

Amy felt a pang of jealousy. Her grandmother had taken an obvious shine to Winnie.

"She had to go home to mind her baby brother," she fibbed. Winnie never had to mind Pauley. She only bothered with him when she felt like it. Whereas Amy had been taking care of the boys, especially Harry, all her life it seemed.

After washing up the supper dishes, Amy slipped upstairs with her schoolbag. She had decided to write her letter on workbook paper so she wouldn't have to ask Gramma for the writing tablet. Gramma would have let her use it, of course, but then she would have insisted on reading the letter before it was sealed.

Amy shut the door, wedged the back of the bedroom chair under the doorknob, and clicked on the Tiffany lamp. Then she kissed her mother's picture, propped herself up on the pillows against the iron bedrail, put her schoolbag on her lap for a desk, and began to write.

April 20, 1926

Dear Aunt Bessie,

How are you and Uncle Wallace and

Janey? Fine I hope. We are all fine here in the purple house. I guess Gramma already told you that our Harry was very sick a few weeks ago and had to have the doctor."

Amy stopped, remembering that awful afternoon. A cold shiver passed through her body and she pulled the quilt up over her knees.

But he is all better now and is back to school. Mike and Pat are fine and so are Gramma and me. My dad is fine also.

My best friend's name is Winnie Plum. Her mother is really nice and pretty and she has a cute baby brother named Paul after their father. But Winnie nicknamed him Pauley so they wouldn't have to call him Junior. Mr. Plum works in a bank and I think they are rich. They have nice furniture, a piano, and a Hupmobile motor-car."

Amy paused again and chewed the pink eraser at the end of her pencil. She couldn't think what else to say to someone she hadn't seen for over six years.

Well, I better go now and do my homework. I get good marks in school. Better than the boys. Gramma says my marks don't matter because girls don't need a good schooling because they are only going to be housewives and mothers when they grow up.

*So she is always after Mike and Pat to beat
me. But they never do!*

*Anyway, I have already decided not to be
a housewife because it is too much work. So
I am going to be a teacher or a writer when I
grow up. My teacher, Mr. Daniels, who is
handsome and nice, says my stories are ex-
cellent.*

Amy stopped and read over what she had written. She frowned as she read the last part.

*Aunt Bessie, when you write back to me I
will appreciate it if you do not mention my
ambitions. You see Gramma wouldn't understand.*

*The main reason I am writing this letter
is to ask you for a picture of Janey. I want to
show it to Winnie and her mother. And I want
to see for myself what my little sister looks
like.*

> *Thanking you in advance,
> I remain,
> Your obedient niece,
> Amy Phair.*

Hiding the workbook under her pillow, Amy
went downstairs. Gramma was sitting on a chair
under the kitchen's dangling light fixture. Socks
were piled up on the table beside the sewing-basket

and she was pulling a long black stocking over a burned-out light bulb.

Flexing her thin stooped shoulders, she peered over the top of her wire-rimmed spectacles at Amy. "Ah, there you are, miss. And what have you been up to?"

Amy hesitated. Did she have to tell Gramma she had written a letter to Aunt Bessie? She had a right to write a letter, didn't she? It was the King's Mail wasn't it? Not Gramma's.

"Homework," she answered.

Gramma took off her glasses and rubbed her eyes with a gnarled knuckle. Amy noticed that her eyes were cloudy and bloodshot. Putting her glasses back on Gramma said, "Thread that big needle with black yarn for me, Amy. I've just got one more stocking to mend and I'll be finished, thank the Lord."

Amy threaded all the darning-needles with yarn and the finer needles with thread, and stuck them into the pincushion. Then she went back into the parlour.

The boys were sitting cross-legged on the carpet, raptly listening to a story on the radio. The radio was an R.C.A. Victor, a square wooden box with dials and knobs across the front and a big horn-shaped speaker on top, and it sat on the buffet where her mother's good china dishes were kept.

The old rolltop desk stood in a corner by the window. Amy tiptoed over to it and eased the top drawer open. There she found what she needed: an envelope and a two-cent stamp. Slipping them into her pinny pocket, she carefully eased the drawer shut. She glanced at the boys, but they didn't even look up. They kept staring mesmerized at the radio as if they could actually see the story unfurling from the horn, like a picture-show, before their very eyes.

Amy went back up to her bedroom, addressed the envelope, tore the pages she had used out of the workbook, slipped the letter into the envelope, licked and sealed it, stuck the stamp on and hid it in her schoolbag.

Then she undressed quickly and tried to get to sleep before Gramma came up. She had hoped that when Harry got better and was back in his own cot in the boys' room that Gramma would go back to sleeping on the davenport. But she hadn't. "The springs in that old couch poke between my bones like an ice pick," Gramma had complained. "No, this here bed is softer and more to my liking, so here I stay."

On the way to school the next day Amy mailed the letter.

A few weeks later, on a pretty May morning,

Aunt Bessie's reply arrived in the early mail.

"For mercy sakes, it's for you!" Gramma exclaimed. Then she held the letter up to the light of the kitchen window as if she hoped to see through the envelope. "Why would Bessie be writing to you?" she asked suspiciously.

"I guess because I wrote to her one day," Amy admitted.

"You didn't tell me," grumbled Gramma as she reluctantly handed over the letter.

Amy was about to leave when Gramma said, "Well, open it and read it to me. I've got a right to know what Bessie's got to say."

Frowning, Amy broke the seal and unfolded the one-page letter. She hoped Aunt Bessie hadn't said too much.

Aunt Bessie's letter was friendly and nice. She related all the local gossip and news. But there was no snapshot in it. She said she was sorry but she couldn't enclose a picture of Jane Elizabeth because her Kodak was broken and she couldn't afford to get it fixed just now.

"Our Bessie writes a nice newsy letter," Gramma said, nodding her head in satisfaction.

Amy left the letter on the table and went to school.

Chapter 7

The Invitation

At recess Winnie handed out invitations to her birthday party. Amy's hands trembled with excitement as she opened the powder-blue envelope. The matching blue card had scalloped edges. The words were very neatly printed:

> *You are cordially invited to the twelfth birthday party of Winnifred Jean Plum. The party will be held at her home, 49 Silvertree Boulevard, at 4 p.m., on May 9, 1926. R.S.V.P.*

"Are you inviting boys, too, Winnie?" Amy was thinking of Rupert White. He teased her a lot, and sometimes he made her mad, but she liked him just the same.

"No, my mother says I'm not allowed to ask boys until I'm sixteen!" groaned Winnie. "Would your gramma let you invite boys to your birthday party, Amy?"

"Huh!" scoffed Amy. "I'll be lucky to have a birthday cake, never mind a party."

"Well, I hope she lets you come to mine," Winnie said. "It's going to be fun."

"I'm sure she will because Gramma likes you, Winnie."

⁊⊾ ⁊⊾ ⁊⊾

Gramma Davis was still turning the handle that worked the agitator of the wooden washing machine when Amy came bouncing, all excited, into the kitchen. Clothes were piled up in a huge wet mound in the wicker washbasket on the floor.

"It's high time you got home," declared Gramma breathlessly. "This is my third load and I'm not done yet. Make yourself useful and hang that basketful out on the line while I finish this lot."

Amy glared over at Mikey who was making himself a brown-sugar sandwich on the sideboard. "Why can't Mikey help?" she asked.

"Don't talk nonsense. A boy can't be seen pegging out washing." Grinning at Amy like a monkey, Mike put his thumbs in his ears and wiggled his fingers. "But he and Patty can carry out the tub of clinkers from the cellar," continued Gramma. "Now that the warm weather has finally come there'll be no need for fires in the furnace until next winter, praise be."

Patty was sitting on a stool in the corner with a pad on his lap, drawing a picture. He and Mikey both glowered at Amy as if it was her fault they had a job of work to do.

Amy heaved the washbasket off the floor with a huge grunt and glowered back at them.

By the time the washing was all pegged out and the wash-tubs emptied, pail by pail, in the back-yard, it was time to get supper started.

"You, Michael and Patrick!" Gramma cried. "Look alive and help me get this monster out of the road."

They all knew how important it was to have the washer pushed back into the corner and the supper on the table before their father emerged from his den. If he should come out while the washer was still sitting in a soapy puddle in the middle of the linoleum he'd stomp around, complaining about the mess and demanding his supper.

But today Gramma was one jump ahead of him. She already had a stew simmering in the big iron kettle on the gas range.

"Make haste, Amy, and lay the table," Gramma said as she hacked a loaf of bread into thick slices and set them, still on the cutting-board, in the middle of the table.

They were all settled in their places when their dad appeared at exactly six o'clock. Plunking himself with a grunt into his armchair, he noisily wolfed down the stew and cleaned his plate with a heel of bread.

Without looking at him directly, Amy watched everything he did. When he was finished his supper he scraped back his chair, splashed his face at the kitchen pump, and dried on the teatowel hanging above the stove. (Gramma loathed that bad habit and changed the towel for a clean one the minute his back was turned.)

He was on his way through the parlour to the front door when Amy suddenly called after him, "Goodbye, Daddy. Don't work too hard!" It bothered her that he always left for work without anybody saying goodbye.

He turned in the doorway and gave Amy a sharp glance. Then all of a sudden he winked at her and was gone before she had a chance to wink back.

After the boys had gone up to bed and Gramma was sitting in the leather rocking chair, rubbing camphorated oil into her swollen knuckles, Amy got up from the dining-room table where she had been doing her homework. She took the blue envelope out of her schoolbag.

"What's that you've got?" asked Gramma.

"It's an invitation to Winnie's birthday party. I'll read it to you, Gramma."

When she had finished reading it her grandmother said, "Do you want to go?"

"Yes, but . . . "

"But what?"

"I haven't got any money to buy Winnie a present."

"Well, just leave it to me. I'll think of something."

"Then it's alright if I write Winnie an R.S.V.P. and say I'm coming?"

"Of course it's alright. She's a lovely little lass. Pretty as a picture, too."

"Thank you, Gramma. Goodnight, Gramma." She ran straight upstairs to bed so she would have time to write in her T-book before Gramma came up.

"Dear Mama," she wrote. "I am going to Winnie's party and Gramma is going to find me a present. Happily! Amy Phair."

Then she sat on the edge of the bed in her nightdress to brush her hair. Winnie's mother said that if you gave your hair fifty strokes every night it would grow thick and shiny.

When she was finished Amy tipped the dresser mirror and looked at herself critically. Her hair was fine and straight and mousey-coloured, but it did look a bit thicker and shinier after the brushing. Her eyes were smoky grey and they seemed to be squeezed between her round cheeks and pudgy nose like two raisins in a dough-dad. Winnie had long, gold ringlets and a heart-shaped face and eyes as blue as the sky. Gramma Davis never missed a chance to say how pretty Winnie was. If Amy hadn't liked Winnie so much she would have been terribly jealous of her.

❧ ❧ ❧

The party was on Saturday, and by Wednesday Amy still didn't have a present.

"I can't go if I don't have a present. Everybody will have a present for Winnie," worried Amy. "You promised you'd think of something, Gramma, and now it's too late."

"Oh, bosh!" snapped Gramma and she left the room.

"You can give her my pencil-box if you like, Amy," offered Mike. "Pencil-boxes are more for girls anyway."

"But it's not new. I want to give her something new."

Harry popped up from under the table where he was playing with cars made from matchboxes. "I've still got the shinplaster I got for my birthday," he said. "You can have it, Amy."

"Oh, thank you, Harry. That's nice. But I can't take your money." Amy was pretty sure Harry didn't understand the value of a shinplaster. You could buy a lot of things with twenty-five cents.

"I've got a bag of allies, Amy," offered Patrick, putting the finishing touches on his latest painting. "There's cat's eyes and smokeys and agates and dibs."

"Aw, thank you, Patty." Amy was surprised and touched by her brothers' generosity. "But I've already picked out something special."

Just then Gramma returned with a knitting-bag over her arm. Delving into it, she drew out a faded old pullover that had once been pink. "I'll unravel this for you and you can knit Winnie up a vest," she said.

"Eeuw!" Amy wrinkled her nose in disgust. "I haven't got time to knit anything. And besides, I know what I want to give Winnie. An autograph album. I've already made up a verse to put in it."

"Piffle!" sniffed Gramma, stuffing the pullover back into the bag. "You're as pig-headed as that one in there." She darted a disdainful glance into the parlour at the den door. "And you look like him, too, when you set your mouth like that."

Amy knew that wasn't a compliment. But the insult made her all the more determined. She had seen the album she liked in the five-and-ten-cent store. It was leather-bound with pink embossed flowers on it. But it cost twenty-five cents. Maybe she should borrow Harry's shinplaster after all. But where would she get the money to pay him back? Not from Gramma, that's for sure. So she decided to ask her father.

On Friday morning, the day before the party, Amy got up early to catch her father before he went to bed. He was on the red-eye shift this week, from midnight until dawn.

"Good morning, Daddy," she said cheerfully as she helped him off with his coat.

"What are you after this time?" asked her father suspiciously. "You've got your new shoes, so what more could you want?"

It's now or never, thought Amy.

"Winnie Plum, who is my best friend, is having her birthday party tomorrow and I'm invited but I haven't got a present for her."

"And how much is that going to cost me? I'm not made of money you know."

"I want to buy her an autograph album for twenty-five cents. And I've already written a verse to put in it."

He took off his cap and hung it on top of his coat on the wall-rack. "That's a lot of money for doing nothing," he muttered.

Amy felt the hair on the back of her neck bristle. "It's not for nothing, Daddy. I do lots of work for no pay. I take care of Harry, and I help Gramma with the chores, and I peg out the washing. And I do the dishes every day before I go to school."

She stopped, breathless, hoping she hadn't gone too far. But much to her relief he reached into his pocket and pulled out a quarter. "Here," he said gruffly, putting the money in her hand. "You could talk the hind leg off a stool, Amy Phair. And I'll tell that old crone out there . . . " he nodded towards the kitchen where Gramma was rattling pans, "to lighten the workload on you or she'll have me to answer to. The lazy old sod."

Amy knew that there was nothing her dad liked better than to have a reason to get mad at Gramma. So she said, "Thank you for the money, Daddy. But don't be hard on Gramma. She does her best, you know."

He didn't answer, but went out into the kitchen, ate his bowl of porridge, and disappeared into his den.

"Good morning, Gramma," Amy said, as she helped herself to the porridge and filled the boys' bowls.

Her grandmother didn't deign to answer.

She's mad at me because I got the quarter from my father, Amy thought. But didn't she hear me stick up for her at the same time?

▪ ▪ ▪

After school Amy dropped Harry off at the purple house, waited until he went inside, then headed straight for the five-and-ten-cent store on Queen Street. As luck would have it, Winnie had stayed late for volleyball practice. Mr. Daniels had chosen Amy for the team, too, but Gramma had said she couldn't be staying late at school. "You have your work cut out for you at home," she had said tartly, "and there's nothing to be gained from throwing a ball over a silly net."

Amy purchased the album, thankful that no-one else had bought it in the meantime, and hurried right home.

Gramma was spreading newspapers on the kitchen floor and the nice clean smell of Hawe's floor-wax drifted up from underneath.

"Where on earth have you been?" scolded Gramma, rubbing the small of her back as she straightened up. "I could have used some help with that heavy floor-polisher."

Why does she always have to be mad and spoil everything, Amy thought. Then she opened the box and showed Gramma the album to distract her.

Wiping her hands on her apron, Gramma Davis took the album and felt the pink embossed flowers on the cover, as if she were seeing it with her fingers. "It's very nice," she said.

Those few kind words made Amy feel a lot better.

That night she wrote the poem she had composed on the first page in fancy script. Then she copied it in her T-book.

When Gramma came up to bed Amy still had the light on. She turned her face to the wall to give Gramma her privacy. But after Gramma climbed into bed she surprised Amy by saying, "Read me your verse."

So Amy read:

May 9, 1926.

ODE TO A BEST FRIEND

I've often dreamed, throughout my life
Of a sister just like you.
And now I know, dear Winnie
That my dream has just come true.
Love from your devoted friend,
Amy Phair.

Gramma smacked her toothless gums, tied her nightcap under her chin and switched off the light. "That's pretty," she said.

Twice in one day she had said something nice. Amy's heart soared like a bird on the wing.

Chapter 8

A Natural-Born Talent

Winnie's party was a huge success. All four of her grandparents were there, and her aunts and uncles and cousins as well as her school-friends.

But the person that caught Amy's eye was Winnie's father.

Mr. Plum was very handsome. He wore a red tie and a grey striped suit, and the creases in his trousers were as sharp as a razor-blade. He had curly, taffy-coloured hair, a reddish pencil moustache and eyes as blue as the lake on a clear day. It was easy to see who Winnie took after.

All afternoon he entertained on the piano. He played beautiful songs like "Tiptoe Through the Tulips" and "My Wild Irish Rose."

Fascinated, Amy never left his side as his long

fingers floated back and forth over the keyboard.

Suddenly Mr. Plum twisted around on the piano bench. "How about a game of musical chairs?" he suggested. There was a lot of squealing and scraping of chairs. "Now . . . everybody ready?"

"Just a minute, Daddy!" Winnie cried from the head of the line. "C'mon, Amy!" So Amy reluctantly left his side and joined the line and they marched round and round the chairs to the tune of "She'll Be Coming Round the Mountain when She Comes!"

It was lots of fun, and Winnie finally won by scrambling madly for the last empty chair.

But as soon as the game was over, Amy returned to Mr. Plum's side. Turning to smile at her without missing a note, Mr. Plum said, "Would you like to play something, my dear?"

"I don't know how. But I'd love to learn," Amy replied.

Getting up, he motioned her to take his place on the piano bench. Then he reached his long arms around her and spread his fingers on the keys. "Now place your hands on top of mine," he instructed. Her heart in her mouth, Amy did as he said, and slowly, their fingers began to move together.

As the last note floated through the air Mrs. Plum poked her head in from the kitchen. "Paul," she called to her husband. "Would you come out here for a minute?"

Mr. Plum laughed. "Duty calls," he said, and followed his wife into the kitchen.

The girls had formed a circle in the parlour and were playing another game but Amy stayed at the piano, caressing the ivory keys.

Stirring in the back of her mind was a song her mother used to sing: "My Bonnie Lies Over the Ocean." She began to pick at the keys, but her fingers were all thumbs and she kept hitting the wrong notes. Then, little by little, her fingers found the right keys and the tune began to emerge. All at once she realized she had it! A thrill went quivering down her arms and through her fingertips.

She nearly jumped out of her skin when Mr. Plum remarked in a surprised voice, "I thought you said you couldn't play, my dear." He had returned from the kitchen and was standing behind her.

"Oh, I can't!" Amy's face went red as a beet, as if she had been caught cheating. She lifted her hands off the keyboard and laced them together on her lap.

"Have you ever had a lesson?" asked Mr. Plum curiously.

"No, never," whispered Amy.

"Then you play by ear, which means you have a

natural-born talent. You must ask your parents about lessons."

Amy winced at the word "parents." Then she slid self-consciously off the bench and went to join the girls in the parlour.

The grandfathers were in the corner squabbling over whose job it was to wind up the Victrola. Finally they agreed that one would turn the handle while the other put the records on.

Out of the horn-shaped speaker came a sweet tenor voice singing, "Memories, memories, dreams of love so true . . . " Winnie's parents were the first couple on the floor. For one magical moment Amy saw her own parents dancing, her mother smiling up into her father's handsome face, her skirt billowing out behind her.

Mr. Plum danced with everybody, but he saved the last dance for Winnie. They made a beautiful picture, Winnie and her father, waltzing around the room together. But Amy could hardly see them through the blur of tears.

When the dancing was over, Mrs. Plum went into the kitchen and came back carrying a cake with smooth pink icing, silver balls and coloured candles. Mr. Plum sat down at the piano and they all sang, "Happy Birthday, dear Winnie!"

Too soon the party was over, and since it was still

daylight Winnie was allowed to walk Amy home.

"Thank you for the album, Amy. It's my favourite present. Especially the verse."

"You're welcome, Winnie, and thanks for inviting me to your party. I was wishing it would never end." They were standing in front of the purple house, talking, when all of a sudden Amy gushed, "Oh, Winnie, your father is so wonderful!"

Winnie hung her head and went strangely quiet. Then she said, in a peculiar voice, "He wasn't always so wonderful."

Amy gave her a puzzled look. "What do you mean, Winnie?"

But before Winnie had time to answer Gramma Davis appeared at the front door of the purple house and called Amy in.

That night Amy went to bed before her gramma came up so she would have time to write in her T-book.

"Dear Mama," she wrote, "Today was Winnie's birthday. She is twelve years old. Her party was lots of fun and she said she liked my present best of all, especially the verse because I wrote it myself. I spent most of the afternoon beside Mr. Plum at the piano. I played a piece by myself from memory and Mr. Plum said I had a natural-born talent.

"Mr. Plum is wonderful, and I told Winnie so,

but she said the strangest thing, Mama, she said he wasn't always so wonderful. I don't know what she meant.

"Here comes Gramma! Goodnight, Mama!

"Happily, Amy Phair."

Chapter 9

A Guest for Supper

"Amy." Gramma was filling the breakfast bowls with rolled oats.

Amy pushed her bowl aside and turned the page of her history book. Mr. Daniels had said there would be a test that morning.

"Amy." Gramma's voice crackled with annoyance.

"Yes, Gramma." Amy glanced up reluctantly and saw Gramma's lips pursed in a hundred tight little lines.

"I was just surmising, since you've been a good, helpful girl of late," Amy pricked up her ears warily, "that you might like to ask your friend, Winnie Plum, to supper one night this week."

Closing her history book, Amy picked up her spoon and began to eat her porridge. "Why?" she asked.

Gramma was shuffling around behind the chairs, leaning over their shoulders, sprinkling handfuls of brown sugar from a paper bag onto their oatmeal. "Because it's good manners to invite her back," she said, sprinkling Amy's porridge.

Amy hated that. Why couldn't they have the sugar in a bowl on the table like other people, and sprinkle from a spoon on their own porridge?

"More sugar, please!" begged Harry, holding up his bowl.

"For shame on you, young Harry," chided Gramma, scattering more sugar on. "You supped it right off the top."

"I hate role-dotes," declared Patrick pushing his bowl away and jumping up from the table.

"Rolled oats, dumb-bell," Michael corrected him.

"Oh, you two!" Gramma ruffled Mikey's curly hair and pinched Patty's freckled nose. "You're a pair of scallywags."

Amy winced at the show of affection Gramma gave the boys. She couldn't remember Gramma ever touching her playfully like that.

The boys ran out the door, laughing and poking each other.

Amy finished her porridge, packed her school-bag, and put on her sweatercoat. "Hurry up, Harry," she said, hoping, in all the confusion, that Gramma would forget about Winnie.

But she didn't. "You haven't answered me, Amy," complained Gramma.

"Answered what?" hedged Amy.

Gramma huffed impatiently. "I said, how would you like to invite your friend Winnie Plum to supper?"

Amy stopped with her hand on the doorknob and tried to imagine Winnie coming face to face with her father. What would she think of him? She had only caught that one brief glimpse of him through the curtain that first day, so she had no idea what he was really like: how he came out of his den with his hair standing on end as if he'd had an electric shock, his face all stubbly because he hadn't shaved for days, and no tie to close his shirt-collar over his Adam's apple. And the way he ate, shovelling his food in and chewing with his mouth open and belching at the end.

The picture made her shudder. "No thanks, Gramma," she said. Then she grabbed Harry's hand and ran him out the door and down the walk as fast as his short legs would go.

Gramma squawked after her from the open door. "What's got into you, Amy Phair? Why must you be so contrary? You're a chip off the old block . . . just like him in there." She always referred to Amy's father as "him," and it made Amy mad.

As soon as Winnie saw Amy she knew something was wrong. "What's the matter, Amy?" she said.

"Nothing!" snapped Amy.

Winnie clamped her mouth shut and Amy apologized.

❧ ❧ ❧

When they came home for lunch Gramma was outside picking the pansies that were sprouting alongside the walk.

"Goodbye, Winnie, see you later." Amy gave her friend a sudden hard shove that sent her stumbling across the street.

Gramma straightened up, rubbing her back with one hand and cupping the flowers in the other.

"Winnie Plum!" she called in her crackly voice.

Winnie stopped on the sidewalk. "Yes, Mrs. Davis?" she called back.

"You come hither a minute."

Amy frowned and scowled at her grandmother. But the old lady ignored her granddaughter and smiled sweetly at Winnie.

"Yes, Mrs. Davis?"

"How would you like to come sup with us this Friday night? Amy's been to your house time and again so it seems only proper you should return the visit. You must ask your mother first, of course."

"Oh, thank you, Mrs. Davis!" Winnie looked delighted with the invitation. "And I know my mother will say yes."

Amy narrowed her eyes and darted daggers at Winnie. But in her excitement Winnie didn't get the message. Instead she turned on her heel and ran through the alleyway, her long golden curls bouncing like coiled springs on her shoulders.

For the next three days Amy was moody and grumpy and only spoke when she had to.

On the way home from school on Friday, Winnie chattered away. "What will we be having for supper, Amy? Is your gramma a good cook? Do you think your father will like me? Will your brothers be nice to me?"

Skipping happily along beside Amy, Winnie didn't even notice that Amy was ignoring her.

A delicious smell greeted them the minute they stepped inside the kitchen. Gramma Davis came through the doorway from the parlour wearing her best gingham apron and her gold-rimmed "upstairs" glasses which she only wore for company.

"I thought we'd eat in the dining room for a change," she announced pleasantly. The dining room was the half of the parlour nearest the kitchen. "Amy, perhaps your little guest would like to help you lay the table with your mother's good china while I baste the chicken."

The round dining room table was already covered with Gramma's best embroidered cloth. A bowl of purple pansies sat in the middle as a centrepiece.

Amy glanced nervously at the closed den door. What was her grandmother thinking of, setting the table right outside her father's room?

"Oh!" exclaimed Winnie, clapping her hands. "Don't the flowers look pretty?"

"Shhhh!" Amy pressed her finger to her lips and scowled meaningfully at the dark den door.

Winnie looked hurt, so Amy explained in a whisper, "We mustn't wake my father. He gets really mad if his sleep is interrupted."

"I'm ever so sorry," Winnie whispered back, then they began to lay the table as noiselessly as possible.

The smell of roasting chicken had brought the three boys in from their tree-fort in the backyard. They all washed up at the kitchen pump.

Winnie was fascinated with the pump. "Where does the water come from?" she asked as she watched it spouting, clear as crystal, into the tin sink.

"There's a well under the house," Mikey explained.

"Can you drink it?" asked Winnie.

"Indeed you can," answered Gramma, filling a cup and handing it to Winnie. "The lake water that comes out of taps is enough to rust your organs."

"Mmm, it's lovely," Winnie said. "Nice and cold."

"C'mon, Winnie," Amy took her friend by the hand and led her into the dining room. "You sit here beside me." Amy had purposely placed herself facing the den door, willing it with all her might to stay shut.

"Why are we eating in here?" Mikey whispered to her.

"Yeah, why, Amy?" murmured Patty, glancing anxiously at the forbidding door.

"I don't know. You'll have to ask Gramma," whispered Amy.

"Why are we eating in here, Gramma?" Harry didn't whisper, he spoke right out loud.

"Because we've got a visitor." Gramma gave Winnie a welcoming smile over the carving knife. "After all, how often do we have company? Now pass the vegetables around while I slice the chicken. It's done to a golden turn if I do say so myself."

At that very moment, the den door swung open.

Amy looked at her father, blinked, and looked again. He stood in the doorway, fresh comb-marks in his black wavy hair, his face shaved smooth as young Harry's, his white shirt collar done up neatly with a knotted blue tie.

The smell of a room that hadn't been cleaned for a long time drifted out around him. He drew the door shut quickly.

Blinking several times, he gazed around at the circle of faces. "Do these eyes deceive me, or is there an extra daughter at my table?" he said in a jovial voice.

Amy breathed a little easier, and she heard her brothers exhale in relief. "This is my friend, Winnie Plum, Daddy," she explained.

"Welcome to my castle, Winnie Plum," he said. Then he sat down in his armchair, picked up his fork and knife, and surveyed the table. "Well, well . . . fancy china and a nosegay of pansies and roasted chicken with gravy in a boat . . . you must be a foreign princess to warrant such style, Winnie Plum."

By the tone of his voice, Amy knew that he was just being playful, not sarcastic. But she could tell by the nervous look on the faces of Gramma and the boys that they weren't sure what to make of him.

Winnie didn't know the difference, though, so she gave him her sweetest smile and said, "Oh, no, Mr. Phair. I'm just an ordinary girl."

This answer brought a loud guffaw from their

father and the whole family relaxed a little.

Suddenly he turned his attention to Michael. "How's tricks there, son?" he said in the same jocular voice.

Mikey went red to the roots of his curly hair. "I, I, I don't know what you mean, Dad," he sputtered.

"Well, how's the world treating you? How are you boys making out at school these days?"

"Fine, Dad, fine!" they chorused.

"Have you painted any new pictures lately, Patrick?" he asked, cutting his meat into bite-size pieces.

"I – I – I did a portrait of the King for his birthday." Patrick answered hesitantly. "And my teacher hung it on the wall."

"Good, good." His father nodded his approval. "And how about you, Amy girl? Is your schoolwork going well?"

"Yes, Daddy, everything's going fine for me. And Winnie, too."

From then on the meal went smoothly. John Phair even made his mother-in-law blush with pleasure by complimenting her cooking.

Now Gramma was serving up the dessert. She had made an orange cake with real oranges and the tangy aroma gave Amy a sudden flash of memory. Orange cake had been her mother's favourite.

After eating every crumb, Winnie placed her knife and fork neatly across her plate and gazed around the room.

"Where's your piano, Amy?" she asked innocently.

"Our piano? We don't have a piano, Winnie."

"Well, then, how come you know how to play?"

"She plays?" John Phair's heavy black eyebrows rose quizzically. "When did you ever hear her play?"

"At my house, at my birthday party. Remember, Amy? You played 'My Bonnie Lies Over the Ocean' and my father said you played by ear. And he said that meant you have a gift."

Glancing at her father, Amy saw a wave of pain wash over his face. "My Vinny played by ear," he murmured. "Any song she heard, she could play."

"Aye," agreed Gramma softly. "Lavinia had music in her fingertips."

Their words gave Amy another flash of memory. She glanced over to the corner where the rolltop desk now stood, and suddenly saw the piano that used to be there.

"Where did our piano go, Daddy?" she asked curiously.

He didn't answer for a moment. The room went quiet.

When he spoke his voice was a gravelly whisper.

"I got rid of it," he muttered. "It haunted me like a ghost."

Pushing back his chair he went to the wall-rack and donned his cap and coat.

With his hand on the doorknob he hesitated, then suddenly turned around, took his cap off his head, swept it across his chest and bowed. "Have a good evening," he said. "And come again, Winnie Plum!" Then he left without slamming the door!

Gramma Davis peered over her spectacles at the door.

"Will wonders never cease," she said, shaking her head. "I do believe, Winnie Plum, that you've worked a miracle."

Amy knew by the puzzled frown on Winnie's face that she didn't know what Gramma was talking about. So she said, "Will you help me stack the dishes, Winnie?"

"Nah, nah," Gramma interrupted, coming back to herself. "Guests do not help with the clearing-up in this house."

"Oh, but I'd like to," Winnie insisted. "I'm never allowed to help at home."

Gramma went, "Tsk, tsk, tsk," in disbelief. "Then it's high time you learned," she said as they carried the dishes to the kitchen sink. "And here's a nice clean dishtowel for your first lesson."

After the washing up, Gramma got a deck of playing cards from the sideboard drawer.

"I haven't had a game of cards in a dog's age," Gramma said. "Here, Mikey, you shuffle. Your fingers are nimbler than mine."

They played easy games like Go Fish and Snap and Matches so that Harry could play, too.

"I'm having a lovely time," Winnie said as she took her turn shuffling and dealing the cards. "You're all so lucky. I only wish I had brothers and sisters to play with. Do you play games every night? You probably never, ever get lonely."

Amy and her brothers exchanged funny looks.

When it was time for Winnie to leave she thanked Gramma profusely, and all the children volunteered to walk her home.

Winnie's mother opened the door and Winnie ran up the veranda steps crying, "I had a lovely time, Mama. Amy's Gramma is a wonderful cook and her dad is ever so nice, and he's handsome, too!"

On the way home, in the alleyway, Mikey suddenly said, "How come he was so nice tonight, I wonder?"

Then Patty said, "I didn't smell beer."

His words were like a lightbulb switching on in Amy's head. "You're right, Patty. I remember another time that Daddy was nice. And he was sober then, too. Just like he used to be when Mama was alive."

"I don't remember them times," Patty said.

"Me neither," agreed Harry.

"I do," Amy said, and Mikey added, "So do I, a bit. I think dad liked me then."

"It's not that he doesn't like you, Mikey." Amy grasped her brother's hand impulsively. "It's just that he hates life without Mama."

That night Amy could hardly wait to get to bed so she could write in her T-book. "Dearest Mama," she wrote. "Gramma let me have company for supper. My friend, Winnie Plum. Daddy was very nice and he didn't swear or belch even once. The boys were extra good, too. The only sad part, Mama, was that Daddy still misses you. And so do I! Oh, Mama, so do I! Your loving daughter, Amy Phair."

Chapter 10

A Piano in the Parlour

*T*he summer holidays came at last. Amy and Winnie had both passed with honours. Mike and Pat and Harry passed, too, but not with honours.

The girls had lots of exciting things planned to do that summer but Amy knew she still had to finish her daily chores before she could run over to Winnie's house.

She was sweeping the front walk with the cornbroom, her last chore of the morning, when a truck with wooden slat-sides pulled up in front of the purple house. She stopped sweeping and leaned on the broom handle, surprised to see her father sitting in the cab next to the driver. Then he and the other man jumped out, ran around to the back of the truck, and lowered the gate to form a ramp.

Vaulting up the ramp, her father pulled a tarpaulin off a big object sticking up above the slat-sides.

Amy gasped and dropped the broom.

The two men hollered orders to each other as, with a lot of grunting and swearing, they eased the upright piano off the truck and onto the road. Then, tipping it on end, they began carrying it carefully up the walk.

Amy grabbed the broom out of their way just as Gramma came to the door to see what all the fuss was about. When she saw what was coming she swung the door wide open and stared, speechless, as the men lugged their heavy burden up the steps and into the parlour.

They set the piano upright with a thump and Amy heard a muffled twang of protest from the strings inside the reddish cabinet.

It's alive! she thought, and her heart-strings twanged in sympathy.

"Where do you want it, John?" asked the strange man, wiping his sweating brow on his plaid shirtsleeve.

"Right there in the corner where it belongs. Will you give me a hand to get rid of that blasted old rolltop, Andy?"

Gramma bristled and spoke up for the first time since the piano drama had begun. "That's my rolltop desk, John Phair!" she cried, the wiry grey hairs on her upper lip quivering in agitation. "It belonged to my dear departed mother, God rest her soul, and you'll get rid of it over my dead body."

"Don't tempt me, Missus," sneered her son-in-law.

"I know where you can put it, Daddy!" Amy jumped into the breech. "It can go where the steamer trunk is, at the end of the hall. And the trunk can fit at the foot of my bed."

It was a hard job and they had to stop on the landing where the stairs turned at an awkward angle. But at last it was done and the piano took its proper place in the parlour.

"Try it, Vinny!" her father urged, twirling the round piano stool until it was just the right height for her.

She sat on the stool and, with shaking hands and a pounding heart, walked her fingers lightly up and down the keyboard. The sound was not pretty and she stopped, puzzled.

"Well!" her father barked impatiently. "What's the matter now?"

Gramma Davis spoke up again in a disgusted voice. "Any fool can hear it's out of tune," she snapped.

"Then you should hear it with no trouble," he

snapped back. Then he turned to Amy. "I'll have it tuned for you, Vinny, never fear."

Closing the piano lid over the keys, Amy ran her hand lovingly down the cabinet. "Where did it come from, Daddy?" she asked.

"It was your mother's, Vinny. I gave it to her brother, your Uncle Fred when she . . . when she died. When I heard that you could play by ear just like your mother I went and took it back again. Fred put up a great stink, saying that big lump of a daughter of his was taking lessons. But I told him that since it was Lavinia's in the first place, it was rightfully yours."

"Thank you, Daddy!" Suddenly her father seemed like a hero. Nodding his bushy head he turned to his companion and said, "Come away into my room, Andy, and I'll repay you for your trouble with a draught."

"Don't mind if I do," Andy replied, and the two men disappeared behind the den door.

The minute the door shut Gramma started ranting about what had become of her rolltop desk.

"It's a foolish place to put a desk. There's not a shaft of light in that hall corner. And that desk is a family heirloom. It should be here under the parlour window for everyone to see. My Grandfather Holly brought it all the way from Bristol on a steamship in 1846."

On and on she went, but Amy paid no attention. Instead she dashed to the kitchen and got a bottle of lemon oil and a soft piece of flannel from under the sink. Lovingly she polished the cherrywood until it shone like burnished copper. Then she wrapped a bit of flannel around her finger and cleaned each key with a paste of baking soda. When she was finished, the black keys shone like ebony among the gleaming ivories.

True to his word, her father had a man come out to tune the piano. And for a few short joyous days Amy spent every spare moment picking out nearly forgotten melodies. She couldn't remember having been so happy since her mother died.

      🙢 🙢 🙢

One day the boys were out playing and Gramma had gone next door for a rare visit with a neighbour. Amy had the house to herself and she began to play with absolute abandon.

Out of the mists of memory came the song her parents used to dance to. Even the words came back: "Let me call you sweetheart, I'm in love with you . . . " She sang at the top of her lungs and played with all her might. The house teemed with music.

Suddenly the door to her father's room burst open.

"Stop playing that bloody song!" he roared, and he smashed the piano lid down, barely missing Amy's fingers. "Are you trying to drive me mad?"

Throwing his hands up in the air in a wild gesture of despair, he lunged towards the wall-rack, grabbed his coat and cap, and slammed out the door.

Amy sat on the stool, shaking from head to toe.

Suddenly she threw back the piano lid and began pounding the keys with her fists, filling the empty house with a crashing cacophony of wild and terrible sound.

Then, just as suddenly, she stopped and when the echoes died away the house became as silent as a tomb.

Softly she closed the lid and laid her burning cheek on the cool wood. "I'm sorry," she whispered to the piano, "but I'll never play again."

Chapter 11

A Wonderful
Suggestion

*T*rue to her promise the piano lid stayed shut. Each day when her work was done she just lolled on the veranda swing. Gramma grumbled that it was sinful to do nothing, and the devil would find work for her idle hands to do. But this particular day Amy didn't even care.

Just then Winnie came skipping merrily up the walk.

"What's wrong, Amy?" she asked, with her usual sunny smile.

"Nothing!" snapped Amy. "Everybody isn't happy all the time like you are."

The smile disappeared from Winnie's face as if she had been slapped. She whirled around and ran back through the lane.

Amy could hardly believe it. Winnie had never turned her back on her before. And, of course, it wasn't Winnie's fault that she was in such a bad mood. After a while Amy decided to go over to Winnie's house to apologize.

Mrs. Plum came to the door with Pauley riding on her hip. "Winnie's gone down the street to play with Margie Howe," she said. "Why don't you run down and join them? I'm sure they'll be glad to see you."

But Amy knew Margie Howe better than Mrs. Plum did. One day at school Margie had called Amy a half-an-orphan and her father a stinking drunk. Amy had punched Margie right in the stomach and had got strapped ten times for punishment. So she turned away, dragging her feet, and headed for home again. Then she heard Mrs. Plum call her name.

She turned. "Yes?" she answered half-heartedly.

"Come here a minute, dear." Mrs. Plum had deposited Pauley in the playpen with his toys and was sitting on the top step of the veranda. She patted the spot beside her. Amy dragged her feet up the steps and sat down.

"Now then, tell me what's troubling you."

Amy was silent for a moment. How much should she tell Mrs. Plum? "Well, I said something mean to

Winnie, and now she's mad at me. And I don't blame her so I came over to apologize."

Mrs. Plum cupped Amy's chin in her hand and looked into her eyes. "Let's just forget about Winnie for a minute. What I want to know is what's troubling *you,* Amy Phair."

Amy lowered her lashes to avoid Mrs. Plum's probing gaze. The concern in her eyes almost made Amy cry. "You don't have to tell me if you don't want to," she assured Amy.

"It's not that I don't want to, Mrs. Plum. But there's nothing anybody can do about it."

"Why don't you let me be the judge of that."

Suddenly Amy could hold it back no longer. She poured out the whole story: about the piano, and how her playing had upset her father, and how she had vowed never to play again.

"Well, now, I've got an idea." Mrs. Plum's voice was full of warmth and hope. "Why don't you come over here during the summer holidays and I'll give you piano lessons. I used to be a teacher, you know."

Amy's heart skipped a beat. "Really? Oh, I'd love that, Mrs. Plum. But I can only come in the afternoons. I have to do my chores in the mornings."

"That should work out just perfectly, then," said Mrs. Plum. "Pauley goes down for his nap right after lunch. So you could come over about one o'clock."

Amy jumped up, all excited. "I'll go right home and ask Gramma." Waving goodbye, her heart singing, she ran off home, but in the lane her steps slowed. What if Gramma says no, she worried. Maybe I should ask Daddy instead. He won't care as long as it doesn't disturb him. But then Gramma might complain about me being away from home too much.

By the time she got to the back door of the purple house she still hadn't made up her mind what to do. But the cranky look on her grandmother's face made up her mind for her. I won't ask anybody, she thought. I'll decide for myself.

"Shall I peel the potatoes for you, Gramma?" she asked.

"It's about time you did something useful," Gramma snapped. "You've wasted the whole afternoon lollygagging and gallivanting."

A sharp retort leapt to the tip of Amy's tongue. But she swallowed it and got the paring knife from the table drawer.

Right after supper Winnie appeared at the screen door. She was wearing a big smile so Amy knew she wasn't mad anymore.

"My mother says you can come to our house and

stay all night, Amy, if you want to," she said through the screen.

"Oh, I'd love to!" Amy flung the dishtowel up on the rack and turned eagerly to her grandmother.

Gramma Davis was standing with her thin arms twisted like vines across her flat chest and a frown on her face.

"Tomorrow's Saturday. I can't do all the weekend work by myself." She purposely ignored Winnie, whose nose was denting the screen. "You won't be satisfied until you've put me in an early grave."

Amy felt her blood begin to boil. "You always say that to me but you never say it to the boys. And you never ever make Mikey stay in on Saturdays. And he's bigger and stronger than me and he's only one year younger."

Just then Winnie piped up through the screen, "I'll come back with Amy in the morning and help with the work, Mrs. Davis. Honest."

"You'll need to help your own mother," Gramma Davis answered sharply.

"No, I won't, Mrs. Davis," Winnie assured her. "I never have to do housework. Pearl Piatt, Mama's charlady, comes in every Saturday to help. I only have to make my own bed. My father always says I'll be weighted down with woman's work soon enough."

Amy looked up at her grandmother beseechingly. Gramma took off her wire spectacles, huffed on them, and polished them with the corner of her apron. Then, not looking directly at Amy, she said, "Run along upstairs, then, and get your nightdress and whatever else you need."

Amy could hardly believe her ears, but before Gramma could change her mind she high-tailed it up the stairs, stuffed her things in a paper shopping bag, and was back in one minute flat. Then she did something she'd never done before. She kissed her grandmother's crumply, crepe-paper cheek. "Thank you, Gramma," she said, as she bolted out the door.

"You be sure to be back here by noonday tomorrow!" Gramma called after her.

"I will, Gramma!" Amy turned back to wave goodbye and was amazed to see that Gramma was touching her cheek where Amy had just kissed it.

Chapter 12

Sisters

*T*hat night Mrs. Plum let them make chocolate fudge with walnuts and raisins. She put it in the ice-box to set. When it was ready Winnie cut it into squares and they ate the whole pan while they listened to Amos and Andy on the radio.

Amy and Winnie sat cross-legged on the carpet and Winnie let Amy hold Mittens on her lap. Mr. Plum was sitting in his armchair reading the newspaper. Mrs. Plum was crocheting a doily. Every time Amy looked up at one or the other they smiled at her.

When the show was over and the radio was turned off Mr. Plum told them jokes, one after another, until their stomachs ached from laughing. Amy couldn't remember when she had had so much fun.

At last it was time for bed.

Leaning back on the goosedown pillow, Amy clasped her hands behind her head and looked up at the canopy. The ceiling light, shining through the pink organdy, cast a rosy glow over the bed. "I love your bed, Winnie," she said. "I love your room. I love your house. I love your cat. I love your whole family. I wish they were my family."

"Well, I'm glad you love us, Amy, but you've got a nice family too. I walked home from the store with your brother Mike one day last week and he told me you were his favourite sister."

Amy turned her head sharply. "Mike said that?"

"Sure. And Harry loves you, too, I can tell."

"Oh, he just loves me 'cause I spoil him. And no wonder I'm Mike's favourite sister. I'm the only one he's got."

"Don't your brothers remember having a baby sister?"

"I don't think so. They never talk about her. Of course I'm the oldest, so I guess that's why I remember her best." Smiling at Winnie she said, "Anyway, I don't want to waste my visit talking about them. And I'm glad we're friends again, Winnie."

"Me, too," Winnie plumped up her pillow. "I don't even like Margie Howe. But I love you, Amy. I hope we'll always be best friends, even when we're really old, like forty or fifty."

"I hope so, too. Actually, I wish we were sisters, not just friends." Amy sat up suddenly. "I've got an idea. Have you got a pair of scissors, Winnie?"

"Sure, in my desk." She got them and handed them to Amy. "What are you going to do?"

"You'll see. Turn your head around."

Trustingly, Winnie turned. Amy lifted a handful of long blond ringlets and snipped one from underneath where it wouldn't show. Then she handed Winnie the scissors. "Now you cut mine," she said.

"My hands are shaking," laughed Winnie as she lifted Amy's straight brown hair and cut a long lock from underneath. "Now what?"

"Now we braid them together."

Winnie held one end while Amy carefully braided. The gold and brown hair, woven together, was the colour of sun-ripened cornsilk. Then Amy cut the plait in two and they tied the loose ends with ribbons. Finally they held the braids in the palms of their hands, speechless for a moment.

"Now we are joined forever," Amy said solemnly.

"Are we sisters?" whispered Winnie.

"Yes," Amy assured her.

Winnie smiled and fell back on the pillow. "This is the happiest day of my life," she said.

"Mine too. And just think, tomorrow your mother will be sort of my mother, too, but she won't know it." Amy laughed. "And I can hardly wait for my first piano lesson. You never told me your mother was a piano teacher, Winnie. Did she teach you the piano?"

Winnie frowned and pulled at a corkscrew curl, then let it spring back. "I can't play very well, Amy. I think my parents are disappointed in me because I'm not musical. Both my parents are, and they're sure Pauley is, too, because he starts to bounce just looking at the Victrola."

"Your parents would never be disappointed in you. They think you're perfect. I envy you your family. I just love your mother. And I think your father is wonderful." That reminded Amy of something — something she could ask Winnie now that they were true sisters.

"Winnie, you know when you walked home with me after your birthday party, and I said how wonderful your dad was, do you remember what you said?"

Winnie cast her eyes down and picked her fingers. "I said he wasn't always so wonderful," she answered quietly.

"What did you mean, Winnie?"

"Well, before we moved to this house, we lived with my grandparents for a while."

"Your whole family?"

"No, just my mother and me."

"Where was Pauley and your father?"

"Pauley wasn't born yet. And my dad . . . I don't know where he was."

"Why wasn't he with you?" Amy asked incredulously.

"He . . . well, my dad used to get . . . 'like that' . . . you know."

Amy drew in a sharp breath. "You mean like *my* dad does?" She couldn't even imagine the handsome, suave, impeccable Mr. Plum looking messy and bleary-eyed the way her own dad so often did. "You guessed about my dad, didn't you, Winnie?"

"I sort of knew, Amy. Margie Howe said things."

"Oh, I hate her!"

"So do I," agreed Amy's new sister loyally.

"Anyway . . . " Amy rose up on her elbow. "What happened, Winnie? How did he change . . . your dad?"

Winnie's eyes brightened and she smiled. "He took the pledge," she explained.

"Pledge? What does that mean?"

"Well, he promised my mother, if she'd forgive him and come home, that he'd never ever drink anything stronger than black coffee again. And he never did."

Amy let out a big sigh and fell back on the pillow again.

Faintly, they could hear music from downstairs.

"Maybe my dad could take the pledge, too," Amy said. "If Mama was here, I think he could," she added.

"Maybe your gramma could talk to him about it," suggested Winnie.

Amy laughed, but it was a bitter laugh. "My gramma and my dad don't get along very well."

"Has she always lived with you, Amy?" Winnie asked.

"No. At first, after my mother died, Daddy tried to look after us himself. But he just couldn't manage, and I was too little to help much. And he felt so bad, Winnie. Sometimes I'd hear him crying through the den door."

Winnie gulped and her eyes filled with tears.

"Oh, Winnie, I'm sorry. I didn't mean to upset you."

Wiping away the tears, Winnie said, "That's what sisters are for."

Just then the music from below stopped and they heard footsteps on the stairs.

"Let's pretend we're asleep," Winnie said. She snapped off the lamp and they snuggled into their pillows and made sleepy breathing sounds through their mouths.

They heard water splashing and the toilet flushing and then soft footsteps padding into the baby's room across the hall. Then the door to Winnie's room opened gently and her parents crept in.

They went from one side of the bed to the other, and kissed both girls on the cheek.

Amy could hardly remember having been kissed goodnight. Her mother used to kiss all her children goodnight. Once Amy had kissed her father, but his breath had smelled so nasty and sour that she hadn't done it again.

The two girls spent the rest of the night talking in whispers.

Amy told Winnie all her complaints about her grandmother: how she fussed over Mike and Pat and spoiled them and never gave them any chores to do. How she called young Harry "Pet" and gave him extra treats. And how Amy herself felt unloved and hard done by. "But I'm pretty sure I'm my father's favourite. The only trouble is that he's so unpredictable that you never know from one day to the next what kind of mood he's going to be in."

By the time they finally fell asleep, with their braids clutched in their hands, they knew all each other's secrets.

Chapter 13

Silent Practice

*T*here were pancakes and syrup for breakfast instead of porridge. And right after breakfast Mrs. Plum said, "How would you like your first piano lesson this morning, Amy, while Winnie runs up and makes her bed?"

"Oh, I'd love that, Mrs. Plum. But what about Pauley?"

"I'll put him in his playpen next to the piano and he can bounce to his heart's delight."

Amy turned to her new sister. "Are you sure you won't mind, Winnie?"

"Sure I'm sure. But don't forget you have to let me come home with you and help clean your house."

"But that's not the same!" protested Amy. "That's work!"

"Well, learning to play the piano is work to me," insisted Winnie. "In fact it's torture. My father says

I have a tin ear. See you later!" and off she ran upstairs.

So Amy Phair had her first piano lesson. Mrs. Plum was a good teacher and before the morning was out Amy had even begun to read a little bit of music.

"You're a natural, Amy," Mrs. Plum declared. "Before you know it you'll be playing songs you've never even heard of before."

Her words were music to Amy's ears.

When the lesson was over Amy's teacher surprised her with a gift. It was a long cardboard roll fastened with a rubber band.

"What is it?" asked Amy.

"Open it and see," said Mrs. Plum.

Slipping the rubber band over her wrist, Amy smoothed out the roll on the kitchen table. "It's a cardboard piano," she said in astonishment.

"It's for silent practice. So you won't disturb your father."

"Oh, thank you, Mrs. Plum. I'll practice on it every night." Amy re-rolled the keyboard carefully.

Just then the doorbell rang.

"I'll get it!" cried Winnie, running down the hall. Then she called from the front door, "It's for you, Amy!"

Patty was on the veranda, his nose pressed

against the screen, his dark eyes squinting curiously. "Gramma says you're to come straight home, Amy. I think you're in trouble," he said.

Tucking the cardboard roll into the shopping bag she'd brought her nightclothes in, Amy thanked Mrs. Plum breathlessly.

"Wait for me!" cried Winnie as Amy flew past her.

"No, don't come this time, Winnie," Amy called over her shoulder. "Gramma's not nice when she's mad." Then she ran all the way home after Patty.

Gramma Davis was on her hands and knees scrubbing the kitchen linoleum. Plunging the scrub-brush into the soapy water she turned a furious gaze on Amy.

Damp strands of silver hair were plastered to her papery cheeks. Wiping the hair out of her eyes with the back of her hand, she snarled, "You're a wicked girl, leaving me alone with all this work."

Amy looked at the clock. It was only half past twelve. "I'm sorry I'm late, Gramma," she apologized.

"Sorry, are you? You'll be a lot sorrier if I peg out from overwork and you're left all alone to fend for this ungrateful brood."

Skidding across the slippery floor, Amy raced through the parlour and up the stairs before anyone could spot the cardboard roll sticking out of the shopping bag. She pitched it under the bed, pulled her work smock over her head, tucked her hair under the hated dustcap and ran downstairs again.

She went straight to the broom closet, got the cedar-mop and dustrags and set to work. She worked all afternoon, mopping and dusting. As she polished the piano with lemon oil, the musical scales went lilting through her head. It wasn't until she smelled the delicious aroma of beef stew mixing in her nose with the pungent smell of lemon oil that she realized how hungry she was and how many hours had passed.

After supper was over and the washing-up was done, Amy said to her grandmother, "If you don't need me any more, Gramma, I'd like to go to bed now."

Amy could tell Gramma wasn't mad any more; in fact she sensed that her grandmother was feeling sheepish that Amy had worked so hard to make up for being late.

Gramma peered over her glasses at the kitchen clock. It was only half past seven. "There's no need for you to turn in this early," she said, her thin lips stretched in a stiff smile. "Why don't you listen to a story on the radio?"

"You want to play Parcheesi, Amy?" Mikey asked. "We need a fourth."

"Please, Amy," Harry begged. "I want you to be my partner so I might win."

"I'm sorry, Harry, but I've got a headache." She pressed her fingers to her temple to prove it. Then she darted Mike and Pat a scornful look. They were all bright-eyed and bushy-tailed from playing outdoors all day long. "And I'm too tired from work to play Parcheesi. You two wouldn't know what that feels like because . . . " Suddenly Amy stopped in mid-sentence and looked at her brothers. They looked back dubiously. She remembered Winnie envying her her family. "Maybe tomorrow night we can have a game," she said. Then she went upstairs to her room.

Their room. But at least it was hers for a few precious hours.

Kneeling down, she fished the shopping bag out from under the bed, undressed, slipped into her nightgown, and unrolled the cardboard keyboard.

Hopping into bed she put one pillow at her back against the bedrails and the other one on her lap. Then she spread the keyboard out on her knees and began to practice the scales.

As she walked her fingers up and down the cardboard keys she could hear every note in her mind. Soon she was improvising little tunes, and the room seemed to swell with music.

Just in time she heard her grandmother's grunts and groans as she painfully climbed the stairs. Quick as a wink Amy rolled the keyboard up, slipped the elastic on, and pitched it under the bed. Then she snapped off the lamp and pulled herself over to her side of the mattress next to the wall.

She breathed through her mouth as if she was asleep, and hoped her gramma wouldn't hear the thudding of her heart.

Chapter 14

Sin of Omission

*F*or the next two weeks Amy got up early every day to get her work done. She worked like a Trojan until lunch was on the table, and she didn't complain about her lazy brothers anymore.

Then, in the afternoon, without asking her grandmother's permission, she high-tailed it out the back door.

"Where do you think you're off to?" Gramma called after her.

"Out to play," Amy answered without looking back. But she could feel her grandmother's eyes following her as she dashed across the street. She felt a bit guilty about lying . . . but maybe music was like playing. And anyway, Gramma couldn't very well complain if all the work was done.

On this particular day Mrs. Plum had unexpected company, so she gave Winnie and Amy each a nickel and sent them to the picture-show on Queen Street. That day Amy was late getting home.

Gramma was hunched over the sink, and Amy noticed that her shoulder blades looked like chicken's wings with a bony hump between them. A wave of sympathy washed over her. Poor Gramma, Amy thought. No wonder she's cranky. She's getting so old.

"I'm sorry I'm late, Gramma. What do you need me to do?" she asked cheerfully.

Gramma Davis's neck cracked as she jerked her head around.

Amy's stomach muscles tightened at the sight of the pinched lines pulling at the corners of her grandmother's mouth. Something was wrong. A chill of fear crept over her. She braced herself for the onslaught, but Gramma just continued to glare.

When she finally spoke, her voice was as brittle as plywood. "I paid a call on your precious Mrs. Plum today," she said, her voice reeking with sarcasm. Amy's heart sank. She had been found out. Then suddenly her temper flared.

"Why did you do that, Gramma?" she demanded. But she couldn't control the quiver of her bottom lip.

"I've got every right to know why you're over there every day of the week," Gramma snapped.

"What did Mrs. Plum say?"

"She told me you lied to her, that's what."

"I don't believe you." Amy felt the hair on the back of her neck bristle up. "Mrs. Plum would never say such a thing. What did she really say?"

"She said that you told her I'd given you permission for piano lessons. And you know very well I said no such thing. You're a wicked prevaricator, that's what you are."

Shaking the water off a huge head of cabbage, Gramma Davis began chopping it on the sinkboard with vicious strokes of the butcher knife. Suddenly the knife slipped off the cabbage and sliced through her finger.

She screamed as the blood spurted out, then held the gaping gash right under Amy's nose. "Now see what you've made me do!" she cried.

The sight of Gramma's blood dripping on the floor drained all the defiance out of Amy. Grabbing the dishtowel from the rack she wrapped it around her grandmother's hand and pulled her down on a kitchen chair.

"Leave me be!" Gramma shrieked. "Get away from me, you wicked liar. Liar! Liar! Liar!" Her voice screeched like chalk on a blackboard.

Amy was beside herself wondering what to do, when the door to the den crashed open and out charged her father, his face tomato red, his black hair wild and his eyes bloodshot.

"What's going on out here? What's all that cater-wauling about? Can't a working man get any sleep?"

Instantly Amy changed sides. "Gramma's cut herself," she said, putting pressure on the bloody towel. "I think it's bad, so she might need to see the doctor."

"No doctor is coming into this house," he snarled. Reaching out, he snatched the cloth off Gramma's hand.

To Amy's relief the blood had already begun to clot.

"Hah!" Her father flung the red-stained towel on to the floor. "Always making a mountain out of a molehill. Always whining for sympathy, you silly old cow."

His scorn set Gramma Davis's temper off again. Jumping up as best she could, she cricked her neck to face her big hulk of a son-in-law. "You might just be pouring your bile out on the wrong body, John Phair," she hissed through tight lips. "It's this one here you need to deal with." She pointed her bloody finger at Amy. "You've got a liar for a daughter and unless she's nipped in the bud she'll come to a bad end. Mark my words."

Exhausted from her own meanness, she collapsed onto the chair like a bag of bones.

Now Amy's father turned his piercing, red-rimmed eyes on her.

She felt the blood drain from her face and fear clutched at her heart like a vise.

"Well, out with it. What's the old fool blathering about? And it better be the truth, what you tell me, or I'll whale the tar out of you."

Amy could tell by the look and smell of him that he had been drinking again. She chose her words carefully. "Mrs. Plum used to be a piano teacher, and she offered to give me lessons if I had permission from home," she explained in a tremulous voice.

"What did the old woman mean, then, calling you a liar?"

"I said I asked permission but I didn't."

"Why didn't you?"

"Because I thought Gramma would say no."

"And why would you need her permission?"

"Because . . . " Amy nearly said, Because I haven't got a mother, but she stopped herself in time. "Because Mrs. Plum told me to ask Gramma," she finished lamely.

"Does this Plum woman know you have a father?"

"Yes."

"Then why didn't she tell you to ask me?"

Amy wanted to reply, Because she knows all about you. But she sighed and answered, "I don't know why, Daddy. And it doesn't matter anyway, because I don't want to take lessons anymore."

She felt a sudden rush of tears, so she turned away to the sinkboard to finish chopping the cabbage.

Then she felt herself being spun around by her father's rough hands.

She looked up, scared, not knowing what to expect.

"Yes, you do want lessons, Vinny Phair. You wouldn't put yourself through all this harangue if it didn't matter. Now you go and tell your Mrs. Plum that you've got your father's permission. And I'll find time for you to practice, too."

"Thank you, Daddy." She managed an uncertain smile.

Now he tipped her chin upwards with his coarse index finger and leaned down close to her face. She drew back a bit because of his breath, then he whispered, "When you smile like that you remind me of your mother." Suddenly he turned back to the quaking old lady. "And you . . . " he snarled. "Stop your blasted screeching. That voice of yours drives through a man's head like a nail." He stomped back to his den and slammed the door so hard the pictures rattled on the parlour wall.

Amy's eyes slowly left the door and came to rest on her grandmother's bowed head. The old lady was nursing her wounded finger. Moaning softly, she rocked it like a baby against her chest.

Pity flooded Amy's heart. "I'll take care of it for you, Gramma," she said.

Meekly Gramma held out her finger and Amy cleaned it with glycerine and poured camphorated oil over it. Then she wrapped it in a strip of soft cotton and fastened it with a tiny gold safety pin.

Gramma examined the bandage carefully. "I couldn't have done better myself," she said. "Thank you, Granddaughter."

Then, just as Amy was about to apologize for all the trouble she had caused, the three boys came tumbling in the door and the moment was lost.

Chapter 15

A Big Disappointment

Amy stayed close to home for a few days so Gramma wouldn't have to put her sore hand in water.

One afternoon when the work was all done Amy was sitting on the veranda swing reading *A Girl of the Limberlost* when Winnie came dancing up the walk. Plunking herself down beside Amy, she grinned like the cat that had swallowed the canary.

"Guess what, Amy?" She didn't give Amy a chance to guess. "We're going to my Grandma Summers' cottage on Lake Simcoe for a whole week and you're invited, too!"

"Oh, Winnie!" Amy clapped the book shut. "I've never been to a cottage before. What do you wear at a cottage? Oh, I wish I had a new bathing-costume. Will I need any spending money? Oh, Winnie! I'll go and ask Gramma right this minute."

She jumped up and rushed to the door, then stopped with her hand on the latch. Her father had warned her in no uncertain terms not to ask Gramma's permission for anything anymore. He had made it clear she was to ask him. But he was sequestered in his room and . . . dared she disturb him?

"What's the matter, Amy?" Winnie was hard on her heels.

"Shh, I'm thinking." Then she said, "You wait here," and she shut the door on Winnie.

Amy crept across the parlour carpet. The room was dark and gloomy because Gramma had pulled the green paper shades down to keep out the afternoon sun. The whole house was as dark as a tomb, and it reminded Amy of the day of her mother's funeral. Mikey always steered clear of the parlour when the shades were drawn. He said it made him feel creepy, but he didn't know why. Amy knew why.

Pressing her ear against the crack of the den door, she could hear her father's heavy, guttural breathing inside. She tapped hesitantly on the door. No answer. Gingerly she turned the knob and eased the door open. The air was foul. She covered her mouth and nose against it.

She glanced at the bed and there was her father,

sprawled over the soiled sheets, his arms and legs flung out, his mouth gaping open, rattling snores vibrating his Adam's apple.

She glanced around the dreary room: dirty clothes were strewn around the floor and beer bottles were lined up along the baseboard. They looked oddly like soldiers guarding her mother's picture on the wall.

She retreated and drew the door shut behind her. Then she went upstairs to look in on her grandmother.

Gramma Davis was taking what she called a "catnap" this afternoon but Amy knew she was just plain weary. Lately Amy had noticed her nodding off over her mending, but when she mentioned it Gramma's eyes would pop open and she'd snap, "I'm not sleeping. Can't a body rest her eyes, for mercy sakes?"

Her grandmother lay as quiet as a corpse in the darkened room. The sight of her frail body made Amy's heart turn over. Gramma's hands, blue-veined and twisted, were crossed on her shallow breast. Amy noticed that the bandage needed changing.

What if she did die, Amy thought, the way she threatens to. What would I do about the boys and Daddy?

Drawing the door to, she crept silently down the stairs, avoiding the creaky one, and stepped gratefully out onto the sunny veranda.

The swing swayed and squeaked as she sat down beside her friend. "I can't go, Winnie," she whispered.

"Why not? Did your gramma say no? Maybe if my mother speaks to her."

Amy shook her head decisively. "No, it's not that." She clasped her hands tightly between her knees. "I can't leave Gramma alone for a whole week. Her finger isn't healing properly and she needs the dressing changed every day."

"Well, couldn't the boys and your father take care of her for just one week?"

Amy made a face and shook her head. "The boys are as useless as Pauley. And my father?" She pictured him lying there in his filthy stupor. "He can't even look after himself. No, Winnie . . . " she sighed, "I can't go, but be sure and tell your family, especially your Grandma Summers, how sorry I am that I can't come. I hope your grandparents won't think I'm ungrateful and never ask me again." Amy got up and walked as far as the front sidewalk with Winnie.

"Of course they won't, Amy." Winnie smoothed out her starched dress which had wrinkled from sitting on the wooden swing. "And I'll write to you every day. Will you write back, Amy?"

"Every day," promised Amy. "If you tell me the address right now there might even be a letter waiting for you when you get there."

Chapter 16

Fish Stories

The Purple House On Wheeler Street,
August 10, 1926.
Dear Winnie,

Well, did this letter beat you there? You have only been gone half-a-day and I miss you already. Just as soon as your car disappeared down the street Margie Howe came running over to call for me. I glared at her disdainfully and said I was too busy.

I wasn't lying about being busy either. Gramma made a job list for me as long as your arm. I tore it in two and gave half of it to Mikey. He gave me a dirty look and dropped it on the floor and ran out the door. He has been mad ever since yesterday because my father made him and Patty and Harry get short haircuts to last the rest of the summer. And the barber shaved their heads smooth as a melon! Mikey was furious because he is so vain about his black curly hair. He thinks he's sooo handsome. But Patty didn't care. He says he likes it because now he can wash his head and face at the same time.

After supper Gramma let me play the piano because my dad is on the graveyard shift and won't be home until after midnight. So that made up for having to do all the chores because I played all night until bedtime and the boys missed their favourite program on the radio. It was a ghost story, too, and I would have liked to hear it myself but I couldn't give up the chance to punish them. Which is being a "dog in the manger," I know.

Winnie . . . there is something exciting I have to tell you but you must keep it a deep, dark secret. Promise? I know you will, sister.

Well, this afternoon I had to go to Queen Street to White's Drug Store for a bottle of laudanum (Gramma's sleeping medicine) and guess who I met coming out of the drugstore? Rupert White! He is the summer delivery boy for White's because his father is the druggist. He was just hopping on his bike with parcels in the basket. He said, "Hi, Amy, where are you going?" So I said, "Home." So he said, "Can I walk with you?" So I said, "I don't care," so he got off his bike and pushed it.

Well, here comes the secret part. On the way home through the lane, all of a sudden he stopped, leaned across the bar of his bike, and kissed me! I couldn't avoid it, honestly, because I was trapped between the bike and the brick wall. Of course I slapped his face . . . not too hard because I wasn't really mad . . . just surprised, and embarrassed! But that's not the worst of it. Just then I heard somebody snickering and I looked up and there was my brother, Mikey, at the end of the lane. He saw the whole thing and he started chanting, "Rupert loooves Amy! Amy loooves Rupert!" So Rupert jumped on his bike and chased Mikey all the way home. Then when I got home the first thing Gramma said was, "Why is your face all red, Amy Phair?" I said because I had hurried home. Well, that darn Mikey was sitting on the kitchen stool all out of breath making big smacking noises with his silly mouth. I was sure he was going to tell. But he didn't. And now he's got that awful secret hanging over my head.

Gramma is calling me from downstairs (I am in the bedroom) so I have to go . . . be back later.

Much later: Mikey hasn't told yet so I don't think he's going to. Actually, he is not much of a tattle-tale.

I am writing on the dining-room table now because Gramma has gone to bed. Her rheumatism is really bad lately so I gave her a dose of laudanum to help her sleep. She wouldn't sleep at all without it and neither would I!

I had to make supper tonight and I'm not very good at it. Gramma always does the cooking. I made fried eggs and tinned peas and potatoes and turnips mashed together. Patty gagged and wouldn't eat it and Mikey sniggered and my dad got mad and boxed both their ears and sent them to bed hungry. That's one good thing about being a girl . . . my dad doesn't believe in hitting girls even when he's mad.

Anyway, dear Winnie, that's all my news for now. It must be much more fun to be at a cottage. Have you made any friends? None *you like as much as me I hope. But of course we are more than friends and no ordinary person could come between us. I hope I get a letter from you soon.*

> *With love from your sister,*
> *Amy Lavinia Phair.*

❧ ❧ ❧

Cedar Grove Cottage,
Lake Simcoe, Ontario,
August 12, 1926.
Dearest Amy!

I received your letter the day we arrived. But I couldn't answer it instantly because I was car-sick all the way here and I had to go straight to bed with a terrible headache.

Daddy had to stop the car four times to let me upchuck in the ditch. And once he couldn't stop in time and I stuck my head out the window and made a mess all over the running-board. But that's not the worst part, our leather grip was strapped on the running-board!

We had to stop twice for flat tires and once for a boil-over. I managed to get the rest of the way without upchucking again. Pauley slept most of the way and wasn't sick at all.

Anyway, today I went swimming in Lake Simcoe. It's very cold and clear. In the water I met a boy who is one year older than me.

He is as cute as Rupert White and he teased me by pulling my ringlets. I'm glad my mother didn't shingle my hair when I begged her to. His name is Alexander Ford. Alex for short. He hung around our cottage so long that Granny asked him to stay for lunch.

Finally my grandad said, "Haven't you got a home, boy?" So he had to leave. I walked him to the road, then he jumped on his bike and yelled, "I'll be seeing you!"

My grandad is really nice, though, and he makes good jokes. This morning he and my father went fishing. They were gone for hours and hours. My dad caught a big walleye pike. He was so proud of it my granny said you'd think he'd grown it himself. Poor Grandad didn't catch anything. But he said, "You should have seen the big feller I caught last year. It musta been a foot long." So I said, "That's not very big, Grandad." Then he said, "Where I come from, Missy, we measure our fish between the eyes!"

He tells jokes like that all the time and

keeps us laughing. My mother said, "Oh, Poppy! (that's what she calls him) you haven't changed a bit since I was a little girl."

Well, that's all the news so far. I'll write again tomorrow. Wish you were here!

Your loving sister,
Winnie Plum.

P.S. Don't worry about your secret. My lips are sealed. W.P.

P.S. 2 I told my granny about your granny's rheumatism and her trouble sleeping, so she looked in her "Doctor Book" (it has a thousand pages) and gave me this recipe for Tranquil Tea. (She makes it for herself and it puts her right to sleep.) She said, mix together one tablespoon of peppermint leaves, one tablespoon of rosemary leaves, and one teaspoon of sage. Add two cups of boiling water and let it steep just like real tea. Then put it through a strainer and sweeten it with honey.

Say hello to all your family. And tell Mikey not to worry, I'm sure he's still cute anyway and his curly hair will soon grow back in. W.P.

At the supper table Amy said, "Who wants to hear a real funny story?"

"I do! I do!" Harry cried. And Mike and Pat both said, "Me too."

Gramma nodded and stopped chewing to listen. John Phair kept on munching but he didn't object so Amy got Winnie's letter out of her pinny pocket and read them the fish joke.

Harry looked puzzled, but his brothers howled with laughter so he joined in. Gramma Davis laughed right out loud and her teeth shot out of her mouth onto the table. She grabbed them up and quickly poked them back into place.

John Phair scowled at her from under his bushy brows. "If you can't keep those choppers in your head, old woman, then don't be laughing," he snapped. Then he switched his attention to Amy. "Whose foolish fish story is that, then?" he demanded.

"It's Winnie's grandpa's joke. She says he makes jokes all the time and keeps them laughing. I think it's funny."

Grinding his chair back from the table he sneered, "The man's a half-wit, if you ask me." Then he left the house in disgust.

Amy watched him go. He's "like that" again, she thought.

When she had finished the washing up, Amy searched the kitchen cabinet and found all the ingredients for Tranquil Tea. Then she boiled the kettle and steeped the tea and carried a cup in to the parlour for her grandmother.

"What's this then?" Gramma was sitting under the floor lamp knitting a stocking. The needles never stopped clicking and she seldom looked at her work.

"It's tea, Gramma. But it's not ordinary tea. It's Winnie's granny's recipe and she says it will help you sleep."

Gramma put down her knitting and took the cup between her gnarled fingers. First she sniffed the strange brew, then she blew steam off the top and sipped it cautiously. "It's very nice," she said, smacking her lips. "Yas, very nice indeed."

Amy smiled, pleased with herself. "I'm going upstairs now, Gramma, to answer Winnie's letter."

"Away you go then, Granddaughter." Gramma's voice was almost tranquil, as if the tea was working already, Amy thought. "And you can tell that Plum girl for me that her grandad's fish story tickled my funny-bone."

"I will," Amy laughed. "Goodnight, Gramma."

Chapter 17

Family Picnic

*T*he effects of the Tranquil Tea didn't last very long. "What are you sulking about, Amy Phair?" grumbled Gramma as she peeled potatoes into a newspaper the next day. "You're always looking woebegone about something."

"Nothing," said Amy, who had been in a melancholy mood ever since Winnie left. Then she heard the postman on the front porch. Amy rushed out to get the letter. It wasn't from Winnie, but it was the next best thing. Gramma got a letter from Orillia, from Aunt Celia, one of her three surviving children. Gramma told Amy to read it out loud because her hands were busy making potato soup. But Amy knew that wasn't the real reason. Gramma loved to read letters. The real reason was because her eyes were failing.

"Dear Mama," the letter began. Amy noticed

with a start that Aunt Celia's lyrical handwriting was almost exactly like her mother's. She had seen her mother's writing on an envelope once but there had been no letter inside.

"Well, go on, go on!" prompted Gramma.

Donald and I are planning a little motor trip to Toronto and we thought it would be nice if we all got together in High Park for a family picnic. I said to Donald, it's been a long time since I've seen my mother, and my sister's children. I want our children to get to know their grandmother and their cousins better. And Donald is anxious to take his new touring-car out for a spin and he says Toronto is just the right distance.

Our Robbie is a big boy now, and the twins are finally old enough to travel. Oh, just wait till you see them, Mama, they have grown so beautiful.

Amy knew that the twins, Dot and Daisy, were the same age as her baby sister and already she was jealous of them.

I have been in touch with brother Fred and Moira and they will meet us Saturday afternoon at the picnic-grounds. Also, and I hope I wasn't over-stepping the mark when I did this, Mama, I sent a note to John's brother, Bill Phair, and his new wife, Caroline. Bill told me in a return letter that Caroline is a good stepmother to his three boys and he wishes John would find a new mother for his poor motherless children.

A new mother? Amy wished people would mind their own business!

Moira has offered to bring a potato salad, and Caroline is bringing hard-boiled eggs, so would it be too much trouble for you to make sandwiches, Mama? Donald prefers salmon and my children like bologna best. Donald says he will buy ginger ale and Orange Crush when we arrive in the city because food would spoil on the road.

> *We can't wait*
> *to see you all!*
> *Lovingly, your daughter,*
> *Celia.*

"Celia is a funny name," Amy remarked as she slipped the letter back into the envelope. "Why did you call her that, Gramma?"

"It's not funny and it's not Celia," Gramma snapped. "It's Cecilia. I named her after my sainted mother."

"Oh." It was hard to believe that Gramma had once been a little girl with a mother named Cecilia.

"It'll be nice to see what's left of my ten children," Gramma sighed. "Never did I dream, as a young mother, that I'd outlive so many of them."

Amy felt a pang of guilt, mixed with sorrow, for her grandmother. She pitied herself so much for the loss of her own mother that she seldom gave any thought to Gramma's trail of tragedies. She knew that two of her aunts had died very young, and that Gramma had lost three sons in the war, and one to diphtheria at six months old.

"Are we going to invite Daddy to the picnic?" asked Amy.

Patty looked up from the picture he was painting on the kitchen table. The scowling man in the picture looked remarkably like John Phair. "I hope not," he said, his dark eyes flashing.

"I hope not, too," Mike agreed. "He'll only make trouble."

Gramma glanced into the parlour at the den door. "It might be best to let sleeping dogs lie," she murmured.

"But Gramma . . . " Amy persisted. "If Uncle Bill is coming, shouldn't Daddy come too?"

"Who's going to tell him about it?" asked Mike.

"Not me!" Patty cried.

"Oh, who asked you!" retorted Amy. "I'll tell him myself after supper."

"That might be best," Gramma said. "You can usually wrap him around your little finger."

Amy waited until their father was finished eating supper. He let out a loud wet belch, then, instead of excusing himself, he laughed and bragged, "That was a fine, audible manifestation of enjoyment."

"Daddy," Amy said, ignoring his bad manners. "There's going to be a family picnic in High Park on Saturday and Uncle Bill is coming. Will you come too?"

Instantly he darted Gramma Davis a suspicious look. "Whose bright idea was that, then?" he asked sarcastically.

"Aunt Celia wrote it in a letter," Amy explained. "She says Uncle Donald has a new touring-car and he's anxious to take it for a spin."

"HAH!" he exploded, scraping his chair back. "I knew there had to be a reason. Well, we ordinary sinners can't miss a chance to see the Reverend's new chariot, now can we? I wonder how many times he clipped the poor-box to afford that little item."

Amy had completely forgotten that Uncle Donald was a preacher.

"HAH!" John Phair gave a loud snort as he clomped through the parlour and out the front door. He disdained to use the kitchen door for his comings and goings. He said it was just for children and pedlars.

Saturday morning broke bright and clear and Amy felt herself getting excited.

"I'll make the sandwiches, Gramma," she volunteered.

She worked happily, making stacks of salmon and bologna sandwiches for Aunt Celia's family. Then she made a pile of fried-egg sandwiches because she knew they were her father's favourite.

Dressed in her clean play-dress — Amy had begged to wear her Sunday dress but Gramma insisted that play-clothes were more suitable for a picnic — they boarded the Queen Street trolley.

Amy carried the wicker picnic-basket full of sandwiches and mixed biscuits covered by a checkered napkin, the boys each toted a striped canvas chair, and their father brought up the rear lugging his box of beer. It took two solid hours to get to High Park from Wheeler Street. They had to transfer twice and there was a long wait between trolley-cars.

They found the whole family gathered under a huge chestnut tree and the first thing Amy noticed was that they were all dressed in their Sunday best. The men all wore straw boaters and shirts and ties.

Amy's father wore no hat at all, and his black mop of hair stuck up like a haystack.

Aunt Celia ran up and hugged Gramma Davis. "Oh, Mama! Mama! You're so thin!" she cried. "Haven't you been keeping well?"

"Humph!" returned her mother, grimly accepting a kiss on her hollow cheek. "Well as can be expected, what with the load I carry." She cocked her head towards all her charges.

"Oh, Amy! Amy! What a big girl you've become." Aunt Celia held her niece at arm's length. "You're the spitting image of John's sister, Nellie." Amy shrank at the comparison because she'd often heard her father say that his sister Nellie was as plain as bread pudding.

"And boys! boys!" Aunt Celia smiled at them over Amy's shoulder. "You'll have to introduce yourselves. You've grown so much I don't know which is which."

"Humph!" snorted Gramma again. "It's not much wonder you don't know one from the other. You've only seen them twice since their mother went home."

A guilty look passed quickly over Aunt Celia's rather pretty face. She looks a lot like Mama's picture, Amy thought wistfully.

Now Aunt Celia turned to John Phair as he

trundled towards them, hefting his box of beer.

"John! John!" Aunt Celia seemed to have to greet everybody twice. "How are *you,* John dear?" she gushed.

He stopped dead and glowered down at her until her eyes fell. Then he turned to his sons and barked, "Open up one of them chairs for your father. And the old lady better get setting down, too, before she falls down."

The girl cousins, all gussied up in their pretty dresses, made Amy feel plain and shy. But her brothers hit it off right away with the boy cousins, who had had their heads shaved for summer, too, and Uncle Donald let them all explore his touring-car.

"Dad! Dad!" yelled Mikey, standing on the running board, "Come see Uncle Donald's swell motor-car."

John Phair jumped back up, flung his chair around in the opposite direction, flopped back into it and snapped open a bottle of beer.

Amy heard her Uncle Donald mutter, "Disgraceful!" Then he turned away, as if the sight of her father offended him. Sitting on a bench, he took his twins up on his lap.

Dot and Daisy perched on either knee like frilly pink dolls. It made Amy suddenly angry to see them sitting there so proud and pretty. Janey had never sat on her father's lap.

Her other girl cousin, who was older than Amy, was Uncle Fred's daughter, the one her father had called a "big lump." The description suited her to a T, Amy thought. Her name was Velma May and she hadn't forgotten that Amy's father had snatched the piano right out from under her nose. "We've got a brand-new piano," she smirked, "and it's much nicer than the old one." Then she twirled on her toe and her huge blue skirt billowed out like sheets in the wind, showing off her lacy underdrawers. "Do you like my new dress? My mother made it for me. Who made your dress, Amy?"

At that very moment Harry appeared at Amy's side as if he'd been sent for. Tugging at her hand he begged, "Will you go for a walk with me, Amy? Mikey sent me away and said I'm too little to play with them."

Turning on her heel, Amy grabbed his hand and headed for a leafy path among the massive trees.

"May I come, too?" called Velma May.

"NO!" Amy shouted back, walking faster.

"I don't like them cousins," Harry said, scrambling to keep up to her.

"Me neither." Amy slowed down once they were out of sight of the picnic grounds. "C'mon, Harry, let's find acorns to feed the squirrels."

It was while they were being extra quiet, so Harry could coax a black squirrel to feed out of his hand, that Amy heard it: music, soft and sweet, filtering through the trees like sunlight. Forgetting Harry for a moment she crept down another path and peeked around a chokecherry bush.

There, sitting on a stump, was a man with a beard playing a violin. Amy didn't recognize the tune, but the music was so beautiful that it filled her eyes with tears.

Harry had caught up to her and was tugging at her hand again.

"I'm hungry," he whined. Then he noticed the tears running down her cheeks. "Why are you crying, Amy?" he asked anxiously.

Embarrassed, she wiped the tears away with the back of her hand. "It's nothing, Harry," she said. "I just stubbed my toe."

Just then the man stopped playing and smiled at her. "You like my music, then?" he said.

"Yes, thank you very much," she replied.

"Do you play?" asked the man as he packed his violin carefully in its case and laid the bow beside it.

"I'm taking piano lessons."

"*Wunderbar!* Good luck then, *liebling. Auf weidersehen*."

"*Auf weidersehen*," Amy called back.

"Come on, Amy. I'm hungry," Harry begged.

"Oh, all right," she said, dropping his hand. "I'll race you back to the picnic table." She gave him a big head start so he would win.

When she came in sight of the family, sitting around in groups, she slowed her steps and they didn't notice her as she came up behind the big chestnut tree.

They sat in a circle around Gramma, who was ensconced on the long canvas chair with a shawl draped over her legs. The first words Amy heard were from her mother's brother, Fred.

"It's a crying shame the way he drinks. What kind of example is that for Lavinia's children?"

Amy held her breath and pressed her back against the tree trunk.

"I tried to be nice to him," sniffed Aunt Celia, "but he just returned the compliment with insults."

"Well, he's got nothing good to say about me either and I've never done him a lick of harm," said Uncle Donald piously. "If I was him I'd be ashamed, sending that poor baby out to Winnipeg to be raised by our Bessie like she was an orphan child. There should be a law against such neglect."

Almost choking with fury, Amy was just about to jump out from behind the tree when her grandmother's voice brought her up short.

"He's got his faults, I'll grant you," said Gramma Davis sharply, "but neglect of that baby isn't one of them. Without Bessie asking for a penny for her keep, he sends money every week, regular as clockwork."

"Huh!" Uncle Fred grunted scornfully. "Precious little would be my guess."

"Well, you'd be wrong," snapped Gramma.

Still holding her breath, Amy tiptoed away. Imagine her dad sending all that money for Janey. She felt proud.

Slipping quietly through the underbrush, she took a roundabout route towards where her father was reclining on one of the canvas chairs. Through a hedge of spirea bushes she could see her Uncle Bill sitting on a folding stool beside him. Empty beer bottles were strewn all over the grass at their feet.

Uncle Bill was talking. "You must be fed up to the teeth being saddled with that old woman day in and day out," he commiserated with his brother. "What you need to do is get off that stuff, John, and find yourself a new wife to look after you and the children."

Amy clapped her hand over her mouth to stop from screaming. Again she nearly jumped out from her hiding place. But this time her father's words stopped her. "Sarah does the best she can for Vinny's children, the poor old article. And that's more than can be said for the rest of them cackling hens over there." Amy heard him take another swig from the bottle. Then he held it up in the air and it glinted in the sunlight. "And I'll thank you to mind your own business about my habits." He finished the bottle and dropped it with a clink among the others on the ground. "As for another wife . . . I'll have no strangers in my house."

Amy could hardly believe her ears. In the course of a few minutes she had overheard her grandmother defend her father and her father stick up for her grandmother.

Just then Aunt Caroline, Uncle Bill's new wife, called in a sing-song voice, "Supper's ready! Come and get it!"

When the picnic was over (her father hadn't even gone near the table) and the goodbyes were said, they gathered up their belongings and clambered back onto the trolley-car. Staggering up the steps behind them, lugging his box of empty bottles, came John Phair, snapping at their heels like a mean old dog. "Get away from me, the lot of you," he barked.

Strangers in the streetcar gave him wary looks. Ashamed and embarrassed, Gramma herded the family down to the rear of the car, as far away from him as she could get. Pat and Mike flipped the wicker seat-backs over so they could face each other. Harry curled up on an empty seat and promptly fell asleep. Amy sat with Gramma across the aisle.

Gramma Davis closed her eyes and her head began to bob with the jerky motion of the streetcar. The boys were talking excitedly about Uncle Donald's new automobile. Amy just gazed out the window, but she didn't see a thing.

She thought about what her uncles had said. *He ought to be ashamed! Disgraceful! He should get off that stuff!* And she remembered what Winnie had said about her own father. That he had taken a pledge and changed his life. Could I persuade my dad to do that? Amy wondered. Maybe I could ask Mrs. Plum's advice. Or Mr. Plum. Maybe he could talk to my dad and explain about the pledge.

She tried to imagine Mr. Plum, in his calm and pleasant manner, trying to reason with her father. Her father would probably fly into a rage and throw Mr. Plum right out the door and down the purple steps.

She shuddered at the thought. She would have to deal with her father herself.

Chapter 18

Strange Happenings

*T*he opportunity didn't come right away, though. Other things happened to prevent it.

It started the very next morning, when her father came out of his den carrying a club-bag and wearing a yellow rainslicker and a cap with ear-lugs.

"I'm away for a week," he announced in a belligerent tone. "A week without pay I might add, so you'll have to count the pennies, you old spendthrift."

"Humph," grunted Gramma.

The boys stopped eating their breakfast and stared at him with dumbfounded expressions on their faces.

"What are you three gaping at? Have you got something to say?"

They all shook their heads.

Amy stopped wiping the sinkboard and looked at him curiously.

"Where are you going, Daddy? You never go anywhere."

"Well, don't I deserve a holiday like any working man?" He swept them all with a fierce glare as if daring anyone to disagree.

"Yes, Daddy, but where?"

"I'm going fishing up to Andy Bailey's cabin on Lake Scugog. Andy says there's whitefish up there as big as Harry. Have you any objection?"

"No, Daddy. I hope you have a good time."

Just then a horn blared "Ahh-ooga!" in front of the house. "Well, I'll be off then." Swinging his bag, John Phair marched out the front door, leaving it wide open behind him. They all crowded out onto the veranda and yelled goodbye over the railing.

He waved his hand out the cab window, but he didn't look back as Andy Bailey's rattly old slat-sided truck went back-firing up Wheeler Street.

Amy noticed the change in her grandmother as soon as the truck disappeared from sight. The wrinkles in her transparent skin seemed to smooth right out, and her mouth relaxed into a smile. Gramma looks younger, Amy thought, following her back into the kitchen. Why, she's even standing straighter!

As if reading Amy's mind, Gramma Davis stretched her neck and flexed her shoulder blades. "When I was a young woman my back was straight as a poker," she said. "Now, then, let's make us a nice pot of tea."

After filling the kettle at the kitchen pump, she set it on the stove and lit the gas under it. "Mikey, you run next door and ask Mrs. Tilley would she like to come over for tea." Mike's big brown eyes nearly popped out of his head. "Away you go. And, Amy, you get your mother's fancy teacups from the buffet. Patty, you and Harry clear the table."

Amy skipped into the parlour to get the cups and saucers. It was the first time in her memory that Gramma had asked a neighbour in for tea.

All that day Gramma Davis moved with a lighter step. Then, that night before bedtime, she said, "Wouldn't a soft bit of fudge go nice?"

"I'll make it, Gramma," Amy volunteered. "I remember Winnie's mother's recipe."

When the fudge was set, Gramma cut it in squares, and they all sat around the table to share it. Then Gramma did something else she had never done before: she told them a story about when she was a little girl back home in Scotland. It seemed one night her father had stepped out for a breath of air, and never came back.

Amy gave Gramma a puzzled stare. "What do you mean, never?"

"I mean what I said, never, ever. We never saw him again."

"Well, what did your mother do?" asked Mikey.

"Do? She did what she had to. She took in washing, and my sisters and I scrubbed doorsteps for pennies a day. And my brothers had to stop school and hire themselves out to farmers."

Just then they noticed tears running down Patty's face. "I'm glad you came to take care of us when our mother went away and didn't come back, Gramma," he said.

"Me, too," agreed Harry.

"It's not the same thing," Amy said, rising from the table. "Mama couldn't help leaving us, because she got sick and died."

She excused herself, then, and went upstairs to write in her T-book. "Dear Mama," she wrote.

"Daddy has gone fishing with his friend. And we made fudge and Gramma told us a story. You probably know the story about her father deserting his family. Our Dad would never do that would he Mama? Your loving daughter, Amy Phair."

ও ও ও

The next day Amy was surprised again. The postman brought a letter from Aunt Celia.

"Mercy sakes, two letters in a row after years of silence. What *can* be the matter?" murmured Gramma. Then she handed the letter to Amy. "You read it for me, Amy," she said. "Your eyes are younger than mine."

So Amy slit the envelope open with a table knife and drew out a single sheet of Aunt Celia's forget-me-not notepaper.

Dear Mama,

How are you? We are all fine here. Didn't we have a lovely time at the picnic? Our Robert enjoyed your boys so much that we thought it would be nice if Michael and Patrick could come up for a few days' holiday. Donald is willing to fetch them and deliver them home again. We have a phone now, Mama, 921 Orillia, so you can give us a call if you must. Otherwise Donald will be there first thing Monday morning.

"Can we go, Gramma? Can we go?" cried the boys.

"I don't see why not." Gramma glanced at the closed den door. "Since His Nibs is not here to put the kibosh on it, I say you can go."

"Yay!" yelled the boys.

Sure enough, the touring-car arrived bright and early Monday morning and Mike and Pat went off excitedly, lugging Gramma's grip.

Amy stared after them enviously.

Harry's nose was put right out of joint. "I never go nowhere," he pouted.

"Neither do I, Harry," Amy said, thinking longingly of the invitation to Winnie's grandmother's cottage. Winnie's letters made it sound so wonderful.

In the afternoon Amy was busy pegging out the last load of washing when Harry and his friend Jackie Mason chased each other under the line and knocked the clothes-prop flying. The clothesline drooped to the ground and the wet washing dragged in the dirt.

"You bad boys!" Amy whirled around, swinging Gramma's long flannel nightdress after them.

Laughing their heads off, Harry and Jackie ducked out of reach and the wet nightdress wrapped itself around someone else's head.

"Help!" yelped the victim, peeking out from under it.

"Winnie!" Clothespegs flew out of Amy's mouth and the two girls grabbed each other's hands and danced around in glee.

Just then Gramma appeared at the kitchen door. "Get yourselves in here this minute," she chuckled. "The neighbours will think you've gone starkers."

Winnie laughed and bounded up the porch steps to throw her arms around Gramma. Gramma hugged her back and Amy felt the familiar tug of jealousy.

They had tea and apple-blossom biscuits at the kitchen table. Winnie's suntanned face glowed with excitement as she told them all about her holiday on Lake Simcoe.

After tea, without Amy even asking, Gramma gave her permission to go over to Winnie's house. And she added, "If Mrs. Plum invites you for supper you may stay. I'll manage alone this once because we're just having potluck."

Mrs. Plum welcomed Amy with open arms. Then she handed over Pauley, who was wriggling like a pollywog.

Mr. Plum was still running back and forth bringing things in from the car. On their way back from the cottage they had bought corn and blueberries.

"Would you like to stay for supper, love?" Mrs. Plum dumped a quart basket of blueberries into a pot in the sink and turned the faucet on. Then she added, "But of course you must run home and ask your grandmother first."

"I don't need to do that, Mrs. Plum." Amy wrestled Pauley into his high-chair and patted his fluffy head. "Gramma already said if you invited me I could stay."

"Lovely. Then Winnie, you can help me shuck the corn and, Amy, how would you like to sort the blueberries?"

The berries had risen to the top of the water and were floating around among the little green leaves like dusky blue pearls. Amy picked them over carefully and laid them out on a dishtowel to dry. It's lots more fun helping Mrs. Plum than helping Gramma, she thought. Instantly she was ashamed and tried to blot the thought out of her mind.

When it was time to go home, Winnie and her mother walked her to the door. "We're going to the Exhibition tomorrow, Amy. How would you like to come with us?" asked Mrs. Plum.

"Oh, I'd love to!" said Amy. "But I haven't got any money."

"You won't need any, Amy, because it's Warriors' Day tomorrow and Daddy is a Warrior so we get in free," explained Winnie.

Amy flew through the lane, burst in the front door and cried, "Gramma! Gramma! The Plums are going to the Exhibition tomorrow and they've invited me. Can I have a quarter to spend?"

"Where on earth would I get twenty-five cents?

You heard what he said. He's gone off on holiday with no pay."

Amy stopped dead and the smile dropped off her face. "You gave Mike and Patty money to spend in Orillia. I saw you put quarters in their pockets."

Gramma began rapidly twisting her wide gold wedding-band around her crooked finger, the way she always did when she was considering. Amy held her tongue and waited.

Then Gramma nodded her head. "You can go, on one condition."

"I'll work all the day after," Amy promised.

"The condition is, you must take Harry with you."

"But . . . but Mrs. Plum didn't invite Harry. What if she doesn't want so many children?"

"Well, you run over and ask her. It wouldn't be fair to leave him home all alone."

To Amy's relief Mrs. Plum said yes, the more the merrier.

The next morning Gramma rummaged to the bottom of her handbag and found two quarters. "It's providential he's away," she said, glancing furtively at the den door. "He doesn't hold with spending money foolishly. Now away you go, and have a good time."

"You have to be extra good, Harry, and do as I

say." Amy stopped in the laneway and tucked in his shirt.

"I will, Amy," he promised. "I'm glad you're taking me." This was going to be Harry's first ride in a motor-car.

The Hupmobile was on the street and Mr. Plum was standing with one foot on the running-board. He was wearing a navy-blue blazer with a row of medals pinned over his heart. A navy beret sat at a jaunty angle on his head. Amy knew that this was the way veterans of the Great War dressed for Warriors' Day.

"You three hop in the back," Mrs. Plum said, settling on the front seat beside her husband with the baby on her lap.

They passed a crowded trolley-car and Harry cried, "Ain't we lucky we're not squeezed in there."

"Aren't we though," laughed Mrs. Plum.

Mr. Plum parked near the Dufferin Gates and they all piled out. Then he unfastened the wicker go-cart from the running-board for Pauley, and Amy begged to push it. Winnie and Harry grabbed hold of either side of the go-cart and skipped along beside her. Amy smiled at everybody that happened to look their way, hoping the strangers would think that they were one big happy family.

She needn't have worried about money. Mr.

Plum bought a roll of tickets for the amusements and they went on countless breathtaking rides. After the rides came lunch, mustardy red-hots and sparkling Honey-dew.

The Warriors' Day parade was held at two o'clock. The three children squeezed onto the curb among a hundred other kids. Mrs. Plum lowered the wooden back of the go-cart and gave Pauley a bottle of sugar-water. Clutching it in his dimpled hands, he sucked himself to sleep.

In the distance they heard the band playing "Pack up Your Troubles in Your Old Kit Bag and smile, smile, smile . . . "

"Here they come!" cried Winnie. She jumped to her feet and screamed and clapped with pride as she recognized her father, marching tall and proud among his comrades. Amy and Harry jumped up, too, and joined in the applause.

I wonder why my dad isn't a Warrior? Amy thought as the men went marching by. She considered asking him about it, then shook her head. No, on second thought maybe I'll ask Gramma. She'll probably know, Amy decided.

After the parade they explored all the Exhibition buildings: the Manufacturer's and the Horse Palace, where Harry went wild about the Clydesdales; the Automotive Building, where they had to drag Mr. Plum away from the new automobiles; the Flower Show, where Mrs. Plum stopped to smell every blossom; and last but not least, the Pure Food Building.

"Now you may spend your quarters," Mrs. Plum told them. They each bought a paper shopping bag full of wonderful things: chocolate bars and balloons and blotters and cardboard hats to wear home to show off where they'd been.

Then they headed for the Dufferin Gates. "Oh, boy!" cried Harry, pulling his new cap's green celluloid sun-peak down over his sparkling eyes. "Won't Patty and Mikey be jealous when they see my hat."

The orange sun was hanging low in the sky by the time they reached the Hupmobile. Tired and happy, they all climbed in and lay back on the sun-warmed seats. Amy had to shake Harry awake as Mr. Plum pulled the car up in front of the purple house.

"Say thank you, Harry," Amy reminded him.

"Thank you, Harry," he yawned sleepily. They all burst out laughing and Harry looked at them in bewilderment.

"Don't forget your lesson tomorrow, Amy," reminded Mrs. Plum.

"I won't," promised Amy. "Bye, Winnie. See you tomorrow."

That night, after Gramma had muttered her prayers, dropped her teeth with a gurgle into the glass, and climbed wearily into bed, Amy said, "Gramma, why isn't my dad a warrior like Mr. Plum?"

Gramma pulled the flat pillow out from under her head and punched it up. Then she lay back on it and smacked her gums together.

"Gramma . . . "

"Yas, yas, I heard you." Gramma pulled the quilt up under her chin. "He was a lumberjack in the north country during the war."

Amy digested this bit of news. "Does that mean he was a coward?" she persisted.

"Nah, nah, I didn't say that. He's got his faults, Lord knows, but cowardice isn't one of them. No, he was past the age for conscription, and besides, he had a wife and children to support."

Amy sighed with satisfaction at this explanation. She didn't really know what conscription meant, but she was ever so glad to hear that her father had stayed home to take care of his family.

"Goodnight, Gramma," she said.

"Goodnight, Granddaughter."

Amy pulled herself over to the edge of the mattress and fell into a contented sleep.

Chapter 19

The Operation

Amy was whirling in space on the Ferris Wheel when her dream was suddenly shattered by a crash and a cry of pain, followed by an ominous silence.

She shot bolt upright, her heart racing. Amazingly, the noise hadn't wakened Gramma. And no sound came from the boys' room across the hall.

Just then, through the open window, she heard a familiar, guttural moan. She knew it was her father, but why was he making those awful noises?

Trembling from head to toe, Amy crept to the end of the bed so she wouldn't have to crawl over her grandmother. The wooden lid of the steamer trunk scraped her legs as she climbed over it. Then she ran down the stairs and flung open the front door.

There was John Phair, his legs sprawled up the veranda steps, his head down on the sidewalk. His yellow cap and a dead fish were lying beside one of his outstretched hands.

"Daddy!" She jumped the steps from top to bottom, dropped to her knees and cradled his head in her arms.

She felt stickiness on her hands and, in the light of the moon and the street-lamp, she saw that it was blood.

"Daddy! Daddy! Wake up!" she cried, tears flooding her eyes.

He stirred and moaned, but he didn't wake up.

I've got to get him to bed, she thought. If I can just get him turned around, maybe I can drag him up the steps.

She tried to lift him by the shoulders, but he was too heavy.

"Hold on, Daddy. I'll get help," she said in his ear.

He groaned a little but didn't open his eyes. Under his head a pool of blood was spreading, like spilled paint, across the sidewalk.

Sprinting up the stairs two at a time, she charged into the boys' room and began screaming at the top of her lungs.

"Mikey! Patty! Wake up! Daddy's been hurt!"

"What? Who? Where?" they muttered sleepily.

Shaking them one after the other she begged,

"Hurry up! You have to help me."

Hearing the terror in her voice, the boys jumped up and followed her out. Gramma was standing like a white ghost in the hallway.

"Dear Lord in heaven, what's happened?" she cried.

"It's Daddy," said Amy, rushing past. "He's been hurt."

It took the strength of all four children to drag their father up the stairs and onto the parlour carpet.

Gramma had switched on the light and the minute she saw the blood she spread a newspaper under his head. Then she knelt beside him and gently turned his head sideways. A two-inch gash parted his hair like a knife and the side of his face was badly swollen.

"Soak a clean washcloth in cold water, Amy. Quickly!"

Carefully, Gramma sponged the wound. The cloth soaked up the blood, and John Phair's white skull could be seen for a split second, through the gaping slash, before scarlet blood filled it in again.

"Get me a towel, a clean one." Gramma's lips were pouched with worry.

She folded the towel into a pad and put pressure on the wound. Amy stood behind her brothers, her hands on Harry's shoulders.

"Is he going to die?" whispered Harry.

"Shhh." Amy put her hand over his mouth.

"He needs a doctor," Gramma said.

Suddenly John Phair's eyes flew open. "No doctor!" he growled. He struggled to rise on his elbow, but fell back with a groan on the carpet again. "Help me to my bed," he said.

With a huge effort the four children got him to his feet and half-carried, half-dragged him into his room.

Gramma limped ahead and threw a clean sheet over the messy bedclothes.

Sprawled on his back in his bed at last, he motioned Amy to come closer. His beckoning finger gave her a painful jolt. Six years before her mother had signalled to her from that same brass bed. A shiver ran through her as she leaned over her father.

"No doctor," he repeated in a raspy voice and his beery breath nearly made her retch.

"You need stitches," Gramma said.

"No doctor!" he rasped again. Then his bloodshot eyes closed and he fell into a deep sleep.

"Run for the doctor, Mikey, while he's gone," ordered Gramma. " You too, Patty, there's safety in numbers."

While they waited, Gramma managed to get the bleeding stopped.

At last they heard the front door open. Amy went to show the doctor in, but Mike and Pat were alone, looking white and scared.

"What's the matter? Where's the doctor?" asked Amy.

"He wouldn't come," gasped Mikey.

"What do you mean, he wouldn't come?" cried Amy.

Gramma was at the den door. "He has to come. It's his bounden duty as a doctor."

"Well," Patty said breathlessly, "when Mikey told him it was our dad that needed him he said he'd just as soon jump off a cliff as see that madman again."

"That's sinful," Gramma said. "A doctor who won't come to a man with a broken head. Madman or no."

"Does that mean Daddy will die now?" asked a pale-faced Harry.

"No, Harry," Amy said, but she wasn't sure she believed her own words.

"He's too tough to die," declared Mikey.

"Yeah. Our dad is strong as a horse," agreed Patty.

"You boys go off to bed, now," ordered Gramma.

"You'll only be in the road down here."

Reluctantly, they trailed up the stairs.

"Oh, Gramma . . . " worried Amy. "What are we going to do?"

"Well, we'll have to do it ourselves, won't we? Since the doctor is as big a fool as the patient."

Do it ourselves? wondered Amy. She followed her grandmother into the kitchen and watched as she turned the gas on high. Blue flames licked up the sides of a saucepan full of water. From the sewing-basket Gramma got a spool of black thread, a fine needle and a pair of scissors. When the water reached a rolling boil she dropped in the needle, thread and scissors.

"What are you going to do now, Gramma?" Amy was mystified.

"I'm going to do some mending, and I'll need your help, Amy."

Gramma Davis poured the hot water down the sink, then dumped the contents of the pot out onto another clean towel.

"Thread the needle for me, Amy. Thread it double and put a tight slipknot at the end."

Gramma collected up her tools and took them back to the den. Squinting up at the smoky glass globe on the den ceiling, she shook her head. "I'll need more light."

"I'll get Daddy's torch from the cellar," Amy whispered.

"And the magnifying glass from the sewing-basket," Gramma said.

Amy was back in seconds. "Now hold the glass close to his head and keep the torch steady," Gramma instructed.

Amy braced herself on the bedrail and willed herself to be still. She watched, fascinated, as Gramma poured peroxide over the gaping wound. When it had stopped fizzing, she trimmed the ragged flesh with the sterilized scissors, then began sewing the pieces together. Why, she's mending it just like a stocking, marvelled Amy. Soon the deep cut was neatly closed with black cross-stitching.

"That's wonderful, Gramma!" Amy whispered.

"It's a good job, if I do say so myself," agreed Gramma, snipping the thread.

John Phair snored on through the whole operation.

By the time Amy and her grandmother crawled back into bed a slit of grey light was creeping under the shade. Gramma Davis fell instantly into an exhausted sleep. Amy couldn't sleep for thinking, but she was too tired to write in her T-book. "Tomorrow, Mama," she promised. "I'll do it tomorrow."

Chapter 20

Confrontation

"You stay in bed, Gramma, and I'll make you some tea."

"Thank you, Granddaughter." Gramma Davis' breathing was shallow, and her face was pale and transparent. "I'm plumb tuckered out," she said and her pleated eyelids closed like shutters over her tired eyes.

Amy fed the boys their breakfast and sent them out to play. She stirred her own porridge and stared at her father's door. Suddenly she dropped her spoon and jumped up. "It's now or never!" she cried.

Her legs trembled and her heart fluttered as she walked towards the door.

Gathering up her courage, she made a fist and knocked. Again and again she knocked, but there was no answer. She turned the knob, pushed the door open and crept inside.

Her father was lying on his back staring right at her, his eyes piercingly black in a sea of red. Running his fingers gingerly through his spiky hair, he winced when he touched the stitches. "Who did this?" he demanded.

"Gramma did."

"Not that quack doctor?"

"No, Daddy. Gramma did it."

"Good. What is it you want then, Vinny?"

"I want to talk to you, Daddy."

"Talk, what's there to talk about?"

"About . . . about . . . " she drew in a deep breath, "about those."

Her finger quivered as she pointed to the beer bottles lined up along the baseboard under her mother's picture. "The boys and I, we don't like it when you get 'like that,' Daddy."

"Like what?"

"You know what I mean."

"Tell me."

She took another deep breath, so deep that it hurt her lungs, and the words tumbled out on a rush of air. "You hide in your room and drink. And it makes you mean and you don't take care of us, and we think you don't love us anymore. And we want you to stop it, Daddy."

His eyes flashed with anger and Amy grabbed

hold of the bedpost to steady herself.

"I work every day. I keep the lot of you fed and clothed and a roof over your heads. What more do you want of me?"

"We . . . we . . . we want you to talk to us and play with us like you used to do when Mama was alive."

His eyes were riveted upon her, glittering like chips of black glass. What was he trying to do, she wondered nervously, stare her down? She longed to drop her eyes and run from the room, but she knew if she left now she would never have the courage to confront him again. So she stayed with her hands glued to the brass bedpost.

When he spoke his voice was a gravelly whisper. "I don't know if I can, Vinny."

The fragment of hope in his words renewed her courage.

"You can if you try, Daddy. Will you pledge to try?"

"Pledge! Pledge! Where did you get that word?"

For a fleeting second she thought of telling him about Mr. Plum's pledge. Then she quickly changed her mind.

"It's just a word, Daddy. It means promise."

"I know what it means."

His eyes left hers, then, and travelled to the

picture on the wall. Amy's gaze followed his.

Lavinia Phair smiled down at them with violet-painted eyes.

The room was so quiet that a fly hitting the window-pane made Amy jump. Her father drew his eyes away from the picture and she saw that they were full of tears.

"Is that all you've got to say, then?"

"One more thing I need to know, Daddy." She gripped the bedpost even harder and drew another painful breath. "Why did you give Janey away to Aunt Bessie?"

He rose up on both elbows and cried out in agony. "Do you think I wanted to? Do you think I don't miss her every day?"

"Then why? I could have taken care of her."

"Don't talk foolish. You were only a little tot at the time. And your grandmother was too old to care for a baby. She was already seventy-five years old. She had a hard enough row to hoe with the lot of you, never mind a squalling infant."

Of course.

Relief flooded over Amy in a warm wave. Daddy was right about Gramma. And he said he missed Janey every day, so that must mean he still loves her. And maybe that means he loves us, too.

Letting go of the bedpost, she went to her father

on trembling legs and threw her arms around him. He held her tight to his heaving chest and she could feel the pounding of his heart.

Chapter 21

Rehearsing

*E*very day when her chores were done and her grandmother was having an afternoon nap, Amy ran over to Winnie's.

She had started a brand-new lesson book and she never got tired of playing. By the end of August she had made, in Mrs. Plum's words, extraordinary progress.

The last piece in her new book was "Hello Central Give Me Heaven 'Cause My Mother's There." She had been thinking a lot about her mother since her talk with her father, and she played the piece over and over, singing the sad words softly.

Suddenly Mrs. Plum reached over her shoulder and turned the pages back. "Here, try this one," she said. "I think you'll like it better." The song was, "Just Molly and Me and Baby Makes Three, we're happy in My Blue Heaven," but Amy sang, "Just Daddy and me and Janey makes three."

Mrs. Plum closed the book firmly. "That's enough for today," she said. "Come out to the kitchen and have some milk and cookies. Winnie's on the veranda playing jacks. Call her in, would you, Amy?"

The milk and cookies cheered Amy up and Winnie made her laugh. "I asked Grandpa Summers what school was like when he was a boy and he said . . . " Winnie lowered her voice and twisted an imaginary moustache. "When I was your age I walked three miles to school and back . . . and it was uphill both ways."

Amy giggled and Mrs. Plum hooted with laughter. "Oh, Winnie, you sounded just like Poppy, then," she said, dabbing her eyes on her apron.

Then she pushed the dishes aside and unfolded a newspaper on the table. "I want you to read this, Amy." She pointed to a short column.

Amy read silently.

The Kew Beach Music Festival is to be held this year in Saint Paul's Church Hall on Queen Street. A special event will be a contest open to all amateur musicians between the ages of 10 to 16 featuring three categories: Singing, dancing and piano. The entry fee is $2.00.

Amy looked first at Mrs. Plum and then at Winnie. They were both grinning like Cheshire cats.

"Well . . . would you like to enter?" asked Mrs. Plum.

"Do you think I'm good enough?" asked Amy.

"I wouldn't suggest it if I didn't think so," Mrs. Plum assured her. "But you'll have to work very hard and, of course, you'll need to get permission from home."

"All right, I'll try," Amy said.

She intended to ask her father's permission at the supper table that night. But he complained he had a headache, and to make matters worse the boys misbehaved and were sent to bed without their supper. Amy knew she had better wait for a more agreeable time.

The following night her father didn't come out for his supper at all, and the next night he was in one of his dark, forbidding moods. So Amy decided she would have to ask her grandmother.

She waited until the boys had gone to bed and Gramma was lying on the sofa, resting her eyes.

"Gramma . . . "

"Yas, what is it?" Gramma's faded eyes squinted open.

Amy handed her the paper clipping.

"What's this then?"

"Something I want you to read."

"You know I can't see without my spectacles."

"I'll read it to you then."

When she'd finished reading, Amy waited expectantly.

"Is this one of Mrs. Plum's schemes?" Gramma queried crankily.

Amy felt her hackles rise, but she answered evenly. "It's not a scheme, Gramma. Mrs. Plum wants me to enter because she thinks I've got a chance."

"A chance to win?"

"Yes . . . well, maybe . . . but she says I'll have to work very hard. And that means I'll need a lot more time to practice."

"Well, I can't spare you for long hours. You know I can't manage alone anymore."

Amy bit her lip, but she couldn't stop the tears. Scrubbing them away with her fist, she looked at the den door. Should she have asked her father after all?

Her grandmother knew what she was thinking. "Never mind him," she said. "He's in one of his unholy moods. Read it to me again."

Amy read it again, her heart in her mouth.

"You'll need money for the fee."

"Mrs. Plum said not to worry about that."

"Well, you can tell Mrs. Plum if there's a fee to be paid I'll pay it. We don't take charity."

"Oh, thank you, Gramma!"

Gramma took the paper and folded it into a square. "What will you play?" she asked.

"Mrs. Plum is going to pick out the pieces for me."

Gramma Davis began massaging the backs of her blue-veined hands thoughtfully. "I can see that you're determined," she said. "So we'll have to find a way . . . or make one."

The next morning, after John Phair had finished his breakfast and retired, like a grumpy bear, to his den, the three boys jumped up from the table and headed for the door.

"Halt right where you are!" commanded Gramma.

The boys stopped, startled.

"Archie and Ben are waiting for us out front," Mikey said.

"Ya," put in Patrick. "We're making orange-crate scooters in Ben's back shed."

"And they're letting me watch," added Harry.

"You can do that later," Gramma said. "Right now there's work to be done in this house."

"Housework ain't for boys. That's what you always say, Gramma," Mikey protested.

"Ya. Housework is for girls," Patty agreed.

"Ya," piped up Harry.

"Mind your tongues, all of you." Gramma hissed in a whisper so as not to be heard beyond the kitchen. "Amy has more important things to do."

"Like what?" demanded Patty.

"Don't take that saucy tone with me young man. Now then, Michael, your job is the back kitchen. It needs cleaning from stem to stern. Patrick, I want every mat in the house, and the parlour carpet too, taken outside and beaten over the clothesline. And Harry . . . " She couldn't help but smile at the astonished little boy. "You can help me with the dishes."

"Dishes! That ain't fair!" pouted Harry.

"No, grandson," she agreed, patting his rosy cheek. "But life isn't fair. Else why would I be here instead of your mother?"

🍂 🍂 🍂

Amy threw herself into her work. She practiced at the Plums' house after school, and her grandmother let her play on her mother's piano at night when her father was out of the house. And for good measure, she practiced on her cardboard keyboard.

Mrs. Plum had chosen a medley of Stephen Foster songs for Amy's presentation, and even

Gramma Davis found herself enthusiastically caught up in the whole affair.

One night, just three days before the festival, Amy was playing her heart out on her mother's piano when the den door flew open and hit the wall.

"What's going on out here? Why are you banging on that piano? Can't you see I'm trying to sleep?"

Amy twirled around on the piano stool. Her heart sank. One look at her father's tousled confusion told her everything she needed to know, and disappointment stabbed her heart.

Gramma Davis looked in from the kitchen, and the boys came halfway down the stairs and peered fearfully through the rails of the banister.

"I'm sorry, Daddy," Amy said. "I thought you were at work. I'm . . . I'm practicing for the festival."

"What festival? What are you yammering about? And who taught you to play like that, anyway?"

"The Kew Beach Music Festival. It's this Saturday at Saint Paul's Auditorium. Mrs. Plum taught me the medley. There's a contest, and Mrs. Plum thinks I might win."

Scratching his head, he eyed her suspiciously. Suddenly he snapped his head around and glared at his mother-in-law. "Did you have a hand in this, old woman?" he snarled.

She met his gaze defiantly. "I signed the entry form. And I paid the entrance fee myself out of my own bit of savings."

"*You* signed the entry form? *You* paid the fee? What right have you got to decide these things?" His glare swerved back to Amy. "I thought I told you that if there were any decisions to be made in this house I was the one to make them, not her!"

Amy knew that there was no use trying to reason with him in the state he was in. She closed the piano lid, motioned the boys to go on upstairs, and followed her grandmother out into the kitchen.

Angered at being left alone in the middle of the parlour, John Phair yelled after her, "Did I make myshelf clear?" The slurring of his words made her shudder.

"Yes, Daddy," she answered.

"BAH!" he roared, then he stomped back into his den and slammed the door so hard the whole house shook.

Gramma Davis was sitting hunched over the table, her silver head in her hands.

Amy drew up a chair beside her.

Slowly, Gramma raised her head and Amy was shocked to see rivers of tears running down the deep creases in her cheeks to the corners of her mouth.

"I'll make tea, Gramma," Amy said.

Pumping the handle up and down to get the water flowing, Amy scratched an itch on the back of her leg with her toe and gazed out the window. It was dark outside and all she could see was her own pale reflection in the glass. It looked like a ghost staring back at her.

When the tea was steeped she filled two cups and sat down at the table beside her grandmother.

"He promised," Amy said, sadly disillusioned.

Her grandmother shook her head. "Nah, nah," she said. "He didn't promise. He said he'd try. That's what you told me. Now let's sup our tea and go to bed. My own mother used to say, things always look brighter in the morning."

Chapter 22

One Shining Moment

*T*he night of the festival the church auditorium was packed. Amy, her grandmother, her brothers, and the Plum family (except Pauley) were lined up in the front row. But the aisle seat beside Amy was empty.

Amy was wearing her blue voile Sunday dress and her grey suede shoes with the pearl buttons. She had brushed her long brown hair back from her round face and tied it with a blue ribbon at the nape of her neck.

On the stage, with its lid wide open, sat a baby grand piano. It looked to Amy like a giant black butterfly with a broken wing.

At exactly seven o'clock a regal woman in a black velvet gown, long pearl beads and swept-up platinum hair walked across the stage and rested one bejewelled hand on the piano.

Amy whispered to her grandmother. "Does he know it's tonight?" She pointed to the empty seat.

"Yes, he knows."

The regal woman waited for silence. "Welcome one and all to the Kew Beach Music Festival," she announced in a lilting voice. "My name is Mrs. Doctor Randolph Fitzsimmons and I will be your hostess for the evening." She paused dramatically. "We are honoured tonight to have six talented artists to entertain us: a tap dancer, two singers and three piano virtuosos."

Amy looked past Gramma to Winnie. "Virtuosos!" she mouthed.

Winnie just grinned, excited.

Amy sat back, clasping her hands so tightly on her lap that the knuckles turned white.

First on the program was the dancer. Mrs. Doctor Fitzsimmons accompanied him on the piano. He was a boy about fourteen, who tap-danced wildly to the tune of "Yankee Doodle Dandy." He received a thunderous ovation.

The first singer was a short, stocky girl with a deep, throaty voice. The second was a sweet, petite soprano. Then came the first pianist. He was a big boy with meaty hands and slicked-down hair and he thumped out a crashing march. More thunderous applause.

Amy's heart began to race. Would she be next?

No, a chubby redheaded girl in a pink chiffon dress was being helped proudly up the stage steps by a beaming redheaded man.

Amy glanced at the empty seat beside her, then looked past Gramma and Winnie to Mrs. Plum. "I'm last," she whispered anxiously.

"That's good," returned Mrs. Plum. Then Mr. Plum leaned forward, cocked his head, and gave her a big, encouraging wink.

The red-headed girl played, "Down by the Old Mill Stream." Amy scarcely heard a note. She glanced over her shoulder to the door at the back of the hall.

Just then she heard Mrs. Doctor Fitzsimmons say her name. "Amy Lavinia Phair is our final contestant. She will render a medley of Stephen Foster songs. Amy Phair."

It seemed a long way up to the stage, and the steps were high with no-one to give her a hand.

She crossed the boards on rubbery legs and slid gratefully onto the piano bench. Once again a hush fell over the audience.

She lifted her hands, which felt heavy as lead, and spread her fingers over the keys. She read the name etched in gold on the polished black backboard . . . Heintzman . . . her eyes ran up and down the beautiful ivory and ebony keyboard . . . her heart fluttered in her chest.

The music book was open to the first piece, but Amy didn't need it. She knew the whole medley by heart.

Just as her fingers were about to touch the keys, the sound of a door opening and closing made her look up. Every head in the hall turned as the tall, dark, handsome man came striding up the aisle.

John Phair was dressed in his Sunday best suit and tie; comb marks shone like ribbons through his jet black hair, and his clean-shaven face wore a beaming smile. He walked steadily up the aisle, his black eyes never leaving Amy's anxious grey ones.

Then, with a little nod of his head, he sat down in the empty seat. She replied with a tremulous smile and turned back to the piano.

Stephen Foster's lovely melodies floated out over the auditorium. At the end the audience rose to their feet in a standing ovation. Above the din, she clearly heard her father's shrill whistle.

Amy won the award, hands down: a beautiful miniature baby grand piano on a polished wooden base. Engraved on a bronze plaque were the words: "Kew Beach Music Festival Award, 1926."

Congratulations came from all sides, but it was

what Winnie told her the next day that meant the most to Amy.

"I heard your gramma say to your father 'She might favour your sister in looks, John Phair, but she's got her mother's music in her fingertips.' And your father just laughed and said, 'You're right there, you old upstart. Vinny will never be dead while Amy's alive.'"

From that day forward Amy thought she noticed a change in the whole family. The boys seemed a little more respectful and best of all her grandmother and her father seemed to have called a truce between them.

Chapter 23

The Bubble Burst

All the following week Amy felt as if she were walking on a cloud. She could talk about nothing but the Festival. Even Winnie couldn't get a word in edgewise on the way home from school. Harry, who was old enough to walk home alone now, ran on ahead out of earshot.

When Mike and Pat passed them on the sidewalk Amy heard Mike say sarcastically, "Is she going to brag forever?"

"Yeah," agreed Patty. "She sounds like a broken record." Then they deliberately crossed the street.

"Am I bragging, Winnie?" Amy asked anxiously.

"Well, if you want the truth, you are, Amy. And after a while it gets pretty boring."

Amy stopped under a maple tree, hugging her books to her chest, and stared down at the ground.

A gust of wind sent red and gold leaves swirling around her feet.

"I guess it's over then," she sighed.

"What's over?" asked Winnie, wrinkling her nose impatiently.

Amy looked up and gazed through the withered autumn leaves to the cold blue sky. "Everything. Summer . . . the festival . . . my life. It's all over," she declared dramatically.

"Oh, Amy." Winnie sounded disgusted. "If you're not bragging you're complaining."

"Am I?"

"Yes, you are, and you have no reason to."

Amy looked her friend up and down: her golden ringlets and heart-shaped face and fancy new school-clothes. "How would you know?" she snapped. Then she spun on her heel and walked quickly away.

Winnie ran to catch up. "I understand, Amy, honest I do."

Amy stopped so suddenly Winnie bumped into her. "Oh, no you don't. You don't understand anything because you've got everything. You're spoiled, and you're pretty, and you've got a mother and father and baby and kitten and . . . "

Winnie grabbed Amy's arm so hard it hurt. "I haven't got a gift," she said in a bitter voice that

Amy had never heard before. "My mother says you're lucky, Amy, because you're gifted."

They continued on in silence until they were in front of the purple house.

"Are you coming to my house for your piano lesson, Amy?"

"No."

"Please come," coaxed Winnie. "I didn't mean to hurt your feelings, Amy. And my mother will be disappointed."

The rat-a-tat-tat on the front window-pane of the purple house made them look up. Gramma Davis was beckoning. Amy ran up the walk and in the back door without saying goodbye.

Before she even got her coat off Gramma started barking orders. "You'll have to black the stove-lids. These rheumatic hands of mine can't wield a brush anymore. And we'll be needing to light the fire any day now. The frost was on the pumpkin last night."

John Phair wouldn't allow the furnace in the cellar to be lit until after Christmas.

"Where's Mikey?" demanded Amy. "And Patty?"

"I sent them to the store for sugar. Your father won't drink his tea without his sugar."

Why would they both have to go for sugar? thought Amy sourly.

"Here's the brush and stove-black. Now get busy

and no excuses. I want it done before supper so the smell will be out of the kitchen. *He* doesn't like the stink of stove-black when he's eating."

By the time *He* came out of his den the stove was shining like black patent-leather and the supper was steaming on the table.

Sniffing suspiciously, he looked balefully around the table and slapped the fork out of Patty's hand.

"Does she teach you no manners?" he sniped. "Children don't start eating before their elders. Now pick up your fork."

Patty's face puckered in pain as he picked up his fork from the floor. Amy took it out of his hand, rinsed it at the sink and handed it back to him.

Suddenly John Phair turned on Mikey. "What are you gaping at with your mouth hanging open? Have you got something to say?"

Mikey snapped his mouth shut and shook his head.

"Then eat your supper and shut your trap."

They ate in deadly silence and sighed with relief when their father scraped his chair back, left the table, and banged the front door behind him.

I knew it was all over, Amy thought bitterly. If Winnie was here she'd see what I mean.

After supper she took her music award from its

place on top of her mother's piano, and ran up the stairs to the bedroom.

She heaved open the lid of the steamer-trunk and the heady smell of mothballs made her gasp. Pushing aside the musty old clothes, she set her trophy in a corner. Then she noticed a thick, leather-bound book on the wooden floor of the trunk. She couldn't remember ever having seen it before. Curious, she carried the heavy book to the chair beside the window and opened it on her lap. It was Gramma Davis' Bible.

The pages crackled as she turned them. On the second page were recorded all the births and deaths in Gramma's family. Amy ran her finger down the long list of names until she came to the one she was searching for, written in Gramma's spindly script: "Lavinia Davis Phair, born August 24, 1890, died February 14, 1920."

She read her mother's name over and over again. Two tears ran down her cheeks, merged on the tip of her chin, and dropped onto the page, melting the ink. As she tried to dab it off she felt a lump in the middle of the book. So she flipped through the pages to see what it was.

Pressed in the middle of the Bible was a little square of folded tissue-paper. Inside was a dried red rose and, under the rose, a small white card edged in black. The writing on the card was not Gramma's.

It read: "Love to my Vinny, from your John . . . forever."

Amy had no idea how long she sat there with the rose and card in her hand. But at last she put them back in the Bible and closed it up. As she carried it back to the trunk something else fell, with a little clink, from between the pages to the floor. She picked it up. It was a tintype photograph of a woman gazing down at a tiny baby on her lap. Amy's fingers tingled as she turned the picture over, and her heart leapt as she recognized her mother's flowing handwriting: "Me and my new baby, Jane Elizabeth Phair. My cup runneth over!"

🐦 🐦 🐦

Hours later, Amy managed to slip out of bed without disturbing her sleeping grandmother. Quietly she eased open the drawer of the washstand, got her T-book, and crept into the watercloset.

Shutting the door of the narrow little room she switched on the bare light bulb which hung by a wire from the ceiling. Then she sat on the lid of the toilet, opened the little book and wrote: "Dear Mama, I've been doing a lot of thinking and I've come to some important decisions: I've decided that Winnie is right, I am lucky. I have my family and best of all, Mama, I have the gift of music that you gave me. And Gramma is right about Daddy. He *didn't* promise. But he *did* say he would try. So I'm going to give him another chance. Because, even though he was grouchy at the supper-table tonight, still he looked neat and clean and he smelled nice. Now that's a good sign, isn't it Mama? Your hopeful daughter, Amy Phair."

Chapter 24

The Fall and Winter Catalogue

*G*ramma Davis tore September off the kitchen calendar. "Your birthday falls on a Saturday this year, Amy," she remarked.

"Look, Gramma, look!" Harry was wiggling his eye-tooth, making it bleed.

"Stop that!" Gramma grabbed his hand out of his mouth.

"But I want to get it out and put it under my pillow so the tooth-fairy will come tonight," protested Harry, wiggling it with his tongue.

Amy looked up from the ironing board where she was snipping stitches out of the hem of her school-dress. "Oh, Harry," she chided. "You're too old to believe in fairies."

"Nah, nah," scolded Gramma. "He's got a right

to his childhood dreams. He's the youngest, after all."

"No, he's not, Janey is." It never stopped bothering Amy that the rest of the family seemed to have forgotten Janey's existence. Sprinkling water onto the skirt of the dress, she pressed down hard with the hot iron, but try as she might the sharp crease wouldn't come out of the let-down hem.

"I need a new school-dress, Gramma," she said.

"Well, try to make that one do for a while longer."

"But it's not just too short, Gramma, it's too tight."

"Is there any extra material in the seams?" queried Gramma.

Amy turned the dress inside-out. "No, there isn't," she said thankfully.

"Well, that gives me an idea for your birthday."

Amy frowned. Just for once, she thought, I wish I'd get a surprise for my birthday.

Then Mikey charged in carrying a big, thick book. "Mrs. Tilley sent you the Fall and Winter Catalogue, Gramma," he said, plunking it on the table. "Will you order me up some long trousers? I'm the only boy in seventh grade who's still wearing breeches."

"I need boots!" put in Patty. He was standing in the corner of the kitchen peering through a frame made by his thumbs and fingers. Then he hurried back to the table and continued drawing.

"Me, too!" piped up Harry, wiggling his bloody tooth.

"Well, I need a new dress more than you boys need anything," insisted Amy, putting the ironing board away behind the cellar door. She sat down opposite Patty at the table and leafed through the pages in the catalogue until she came to girls' fall and winter dresses. And there, in full colour, was the very dress she longed for: an all-wool blue jersey with a dropped waistline and a sash that tied at the hip.

"I like this one, Gramma," she said.

Gramma looked over her shoulder. "For mercy sakes, child," she cried. "Where would I get seven dollars and fifty cents for one frock?"

Amy closed the book with a whack and went upstairs. Retrieving her cardboard keyboard from under the bed she began playing "All Alone, By the Telephone." She could hear the melody just as plain as if it was a real piano. Sometimes she imagined she was on the stage again, playing the Heintzman. And sometimes, in her imaginings, her mother sat beside her on the bench and they played a duet, together.

Chapter 25

Thirteen

"Amy, supper's ready," Patty yelled up the stairs.

"I'm coming!" She rolled up the keyboard, slipped it under the bed, and went down.

Her father was already in his chair at the head of the table, both hairy arms surrounding his plate, waiting for it to be filled.

First Amy served her father, and then the boys. "Don't you two ever think to lend a hand?" she scolded Mike and Patty. But then she stopped herself, not wanting to start any trouble.

Supper was finished off with raisin scones and tea.

With a last slurp from his saucer, John Phair patted his stomach and uttered his usual "audible manifestations of enjoyment." Then he squinted at the calendar on the wall. "Well, now, it's October isn't it? Seems to me somebody's got a birthday in

October. How old will you be, Amy Lavinia Phair?"

"Oh, Daddy! You know how old I'm going to be."

He looked at her quizzically. "Ten? Fifteen? Twenty-one?"

"I'll be thirteen, Daddy." Amy couldn't help laughing.

"Thirteen! That calls for a celebration. How about a something special for our young lady here. What do you say to that, old woman?"

Poor Gramma always got flustered when he spoke to her directly. Pecking like a nervous hen at the crumbs on her tea plate, she murmured, "I'll do my best."

★ ★ ★

On the morning of her birthday Amy woke up disappointed. She was thirteen years old and she didn't feel any different. But her disappointment turned to pleasure when she opened her one and only present at the breakfast table. It was the all-wool blue jersey that cost $7.50!

"Thank you, Gramma," she said.

"It's from the whole family," Gramma explained.

So Amy thanked them all, including her father who had got up bright and early for her birthday breakfast.

Gramma set a platter of flapjacks and a jar of

maple syrup in the middle of the table. "A treat for your birthday," she explained.

Mike and Pat raised their forks to spear a helping but their father waved them off with his knife. "Your sister first, seeing as it's her birthday," he said.

"Thank you, Daddy," Amy said and helped herself to the flapjacks.

"What's it feel like to be so old, Amy?" asked Harry, licking syrup off his chin.

"Be quiet and finish up your plate," their father said. "We've got to make tracks this morning."

Amy looked at him, puzzled. "Where are we going, Daddy?"

"That's for me to know and you to find out," he grinned. "Now get a move on, the lot of you."

Slurping down his scalding tea he pushed himself away from the table and left the kitchen. Amy noticed that the linoleum under his chair was worn right through in ragged patches where he scraped it every day.

"You boys run and get cleaned up," ordered Gramma as she cleared the table. "And Amy, you may wear your new birthday dress."

"I think I'd rather save it for Sunday, Gramma."

"I said you may wear it today." Gramma's voice was firm as she turned to the sink and began washing the dishes. "Away you go, now. I'll finish up here myself."

Amy looked, puzzled, at Gramma's hunched back, shrugged, and went upstairs to change.

The dress was a perfect fit. She decided to wear her pearl-buttoned shoes, too, although they were getting a little tight in the toes. Then she brushed her hair and fastened it behind her ears with blue barrettes.

"You've got nice ears, Amy Phair," she told herself with a smile. She tipped the dresser mirror and spun around on her toes to see how she looked. Pleased, she went downstairs to show herself off.

As she reached the landing, her father came out of his den all spruced up in suit and tie, his hair combed back in brilliantined black waves. Why, he's every bit as handsome as Mr. Plum! Amy thought proudly.

The boys were dressed in their Sunday best, too, and Gramma had brushed her silver hair into a shiny bun. She was wearing her black fringed shawl over her black silk dress and Amy couldn't help but notice that the shawl was mended in several places. "You need a new shawl, Gramma," she said feeling a bit guilty about her expensive new dress.

Gramma Davis pulled the old shawl closer

around her bent shoulders. "This one will see me out," she said.

I wonder where we're going? puzzled Amy as they set off up the street, John Phair leading the march. The boys followed in his footsteps and Gramma hobbled along beside Amy, clinging onto her arm.

After a long trolley-car ride they arrived, of all places, at the railway station!

Amy had never been on a train in her life, and she felt suddenly excited. Easing her grandmother's grip on her arm, she sat her down on a green wooden bench. Then she ran up to her father. He was shading his eyes, staring west along the tracks.

"Where are we going, Daddy?" she asked. But he acted as if he hadn't even heard her; clasping his hands behind his back, he began to pace impatiently back and forth.

She didn't know what to make of it. Was her dad really taking the whole family on a trip somewhere? Maybe they were going to Aunt Celia's in Orillia. Amy shook her head. Her father would never spend good money going to visit his prim sister-in-law and her pious husband. What was going on then? Why was her father — and her grandmother, too, because it was obvious that Gramma knew something

Amy didn't know — acting so mysterious?

Amy saw by the railway clock that they had been standing around on the platform for twenty-five minutes. The boys were getting boisterous. They began hollering and chasing each other up and down the wooden platform, dodging other passengers and knocking over suitcases. Normally their father would have walloped them, but today he didn't seem to notice as he continued staring up the tracks.

At last the train came roaring into the station and ground to a screeching stop. Amy felt her heart flutter with anticipation. Her father stopped pacing and Gramma rose from the bench.

The boys clustered around Amy and they all looked expectantly at their father, waiting for his instructions. But he didn't say a word or make a move.

Then, through billowing puffs of steam, Amy saw a big woman in black and a little girl in an unbuttoned reefer coat standing at the top of the train's steel steps. As the steam cleared away Amy saw that the little girl was wearing a pink flowered dress and a pink ribbon bow on top of her dark brown hair.

The little girl looked solemnly at all the people staring up at her from the platform. Suddenly her eyes met Amy's. They were the colour of spring violets.

Amy's heart gave a terrible thud. "Janey?" she whispered.

Then . . . "JANEYYY!"

The trainman lifted the small girl down and the moment her feet touched the boards she leapt into her sister's arms.

"Janey! Janey!" cried Amy, hugging her close.

Then the child pulled back and stared into Amy's face.

"Are you my sister?" she asked.

"Yes, I am! I am!"

John Phair stayed in the background for a few moments. Then he came forward and lifted his youngest child out of Amy's arms.

Staring at him with those violet eyes, she put her hands on either side of his face and squeezed his cheeks together until his mouth formed an O. "Are you my daddy?" she demanded.

Amy's eyes moved from her sister's face to her father's. She saw his Adam's apple work up and down above his shirt collar. He cleared his throat before he answered. "That I am," he said, his voice hoarse with emotion. "And you're the picture of your mother, Jane Elizabeth Phair." Then he quickly squeezed his eyes shut, but not before two tears escaped and ran down his ruddy cheeks.

Now Aunt Bessie, who had been hanging back with Gramma and the boys, came forward to join them. She gave Amy a warm hug and a kiss, then she reached out and touched John Phair's coat sleeve.

"Thank you for sending the train tickets, John," she said.

Amy gasped, clapped her hand over her mouth, and stared into her father's glistening eyes.

"Happy Birthday, Vinny!" he said.

"Oh, thank you, Daddy. This is the happiest day of my life."

Then, above the roar of the train and the clang of the bell and the din of the crowd, Amy clearly heard the words, "Promise me, Amy."

And she whispered, "I promise, Mama."

*B*ernice Thurman Hunter developed an interest in writing in early childhood, and when her own children were small, she wrote stories for them. But it was not until her children were grown up that she began to have her work published.

Many of Bernice's novels are autobiographical in nature, and one of her strengths as a writer is her ability to bring her childhood memories to vivid life for readers. Her books are enormously popular with readers of all ages.

Bernice has received many awards, including the IODE Award for *That Scatterbrain Booky* and a Toronto Historical Board Commendation for *Hawk and Stretch* and *The Firefighter*. Her books have been translated into several languages, including French, Swedish and Norwegian. In 1990, Bernice Thurman Hunter was presented with the Vicky Metcalf Award for her contribution to Canadian children's literature.